Annie Argall

The inspiration of song and other poems

Annie Argall

The inspiration of song and other poems

ISBN/EAN: 9783337175979

Printed in Europe, USA, Canada, Australia, Japan

Cover: Foto ©Andreas Hilbeck / pixelio.de

More available books at **www.hansebooks.com**

Yours very sincerely,

Annie E. Argall.

THE

Inspiration of Song,

AND

OTHER POEMS

BY

ANNIE E. ARGALL.

———

[*Entered at Stationers' Hall.*

TRURO:
NETHERTON AND WORTH LEMON STREET,
1894.

PREFACE.

The collection of many of these Poems in book-form was first undertaken at the request of numerous friends. The venture has since assumed a more general signification in view of the growing interest in Cornish and other verse, but the Author looks only for the support and criticism which can be rightfully accorded. All the Poems must stand on their own merits and unity of purpose.

ANNIE E. ARGALL.

Truro, March, 1894.

CONTENTS.

The Inspiration of Song.

IN a wild and lonely desert, Eve crouched low in
    heart-full grief,
Where the sobbing of the night-wind formed the only
    sad relief
To the dull monotonous silence of the long and
    barren plain
And accorded in its sorrow with her spirit's deep
    refrain.
The day of toilsome journeying had drifted to its close,
And Adam, worn with travel, lay enwrapt in sound
    repose,
But Eve, though sadly weary, was too wrought with
    grief to sleep,
So the night passed with her wakefulness, for Eve had
    but to weep.
Through the day her woman's nature checked the
    sad tears' overflow
And a half sweet smile would light her face, and hide
    her inmost woe ;
In Adam's grief his comforter could bravely crush
    her sighs,

If but to him she might bring back the life-look of
    his eyes ;
And the bitterness of longing, and the sadness of regret
Found in her no outward token while the daylight
    lingered yet ;
But at night when all was silence, and the still world
    doubly lone,
Eve poured out all the agony a human soul could
    own—
Not a selfish, earth-soiled longing, but a great and
    deep remorse ;
Not a simple, childish yearning, but the full and
    anguished force
Of a fallen human spirit in repentance true and strong,
One who knows the height of pureness and the depth
    of graceless wrong—
Such the anguish of her spirit who had once the
    purest joy
God could give His Own created—treasure cast with
    none alloy—
Such her woe, who soiled the treasure with the sin-
    stain of man's fall ;
And in justice was her anguish, who in sinning
    brought to all,
All earth's children through the Future, one great
    heritage of gloom ;
Yet as life is Heaven's grand dower, so the ever-
    pending doom
Was in gracious part averted by the promise in her grief
Of a sure and Faith-surrounded source of God's
    Divine relief.

And the night-wind sighed an answer to Eve's deepest
    sorrow there,
Till the lonely soul of woman lent itself to humble
    prayer,
As the stillness of the desert wooed her into purer
    calm,
And upon her bruisëd spirit fell a soft refreshing balm.
There was not a need of language her petition to
    express,
No words could clothe the agony her soul had to
    confess ;
A breathing of repentance took the prayer right into
    Heaven,
And, before it seemed to enter, the blessing had been
    given.
The breaking of the day-dawn bathed the wilderness
    in light,
But the fairest beams of brilliance broke in glory
    through the night ;
In the darkness of deep sorrow, woe the loneliest of
    earth,
The noblest of all poems had received its troubled
    birth :
In a lonely woman's sorrow human hearts had learnt
    to pray,
And this prayer of deep repentance is our heritage
    to-day ;—
The poem still expressing the experience of all Time,
The word of hope in mercy, and faith in love sublime.

————:o:————

They had reached a hardy manhood, those first sons
    of Adam's race,
In person fully equalling their father's supple grace,
But in heart and inner consciousness fair types of
    that mankind
We know in present circumstance, of both qualities
    combined.
Tall Cain the swarthy gardener, by many a sun
    embrowned,
Was the haughtiest of earth's masters, this tiller of
    the ground ;
His eyes would flash out anger where Abel's smiled a
    charm
More potent than those fire-sparks so fraught with
    careless harm ;
The one would strive in passion, where the other
    sought to please ;
Yet they lived, those early brothers, no life of spoiling
    ease,
For their father's curse was on them, an inheritance
    of sin,
And they worked with strong endeavour God's
    esteemed regard to win.
Abel, the true and manly, was a noble without peer,
Pure, earnest toiling shepherd, who knew no coward
    fear,
Accepted by his Maker, for his lonely generous
    heart ;
But hated by his brother in a jealous anger's smart.
Not at once, as little children, had they drifted each
    from each,

But along the years of boyhood, far as either ken
    might reach,
There was just the creeping envy, with its slimy
    noisome trail,
To disturb the peace between them, Love's enlighten-
    ment to pale.
In Cain's heart the tiny envy grew to bitter awful
    hate,
Soiling, searing all his life-work with the grimness of
    its fate ;
And the gentler speech of Abel, or the pureness of
    his life,
Was but fuel piled to augment the fierce tumult
    of Cain's strife ;
Till there dawned the saddest epoch of a world's
    disturbed records,
When the long-pent fire of passion overturned its
    smouldering hoards,
And the history of earth's people was imbued with
    blood and crime,
To be passed along the ages to the end of finite Time.
How the elder slew the younger in a moment of fierce
    ire ;—
How the murderer had his sentence of desolation
    dire ;—
How the wrath of the Almighty poured itself in
    punishment
On the head of Cain the hater, Cain the saddest
    miscreant—
Is a tale the years have carried down to us in clear
    terse writ ;

And the lives of all the nations have been ever closely
　　knit
With the dull, dark strand of murder, and the darker
　　one of woe—
The hate that leads to bloodshed from the envy lying
　　low—
And the first-born of true Poetry received a sad
　　baptism,
A brother's hate, a brother's crime, its carmine-flowing
　　chrism.

————:o:————

The glittering sheen of luxury had turned to tawdry
　　dross,
The sense of rich possession to a worn heart's greatest
　　loss;
From the height of wealth's abundance to the depth
　　of shame debased,
A fallen, guilty woman lay in woeful grief disgraced.
A faithless wife and mother, she had cast aside all
　　peace,
And lived her life of lawlessness in open careless ease,
Till her beauty lost its loveliness, as her heart had
　　lost its bloom,
And the world she lived to conquer filled the measure
　　of her doom.
Forsaken in her sinning by all who might have stayed
To help her to repentance, they, the *Pharisees*, delayed,
To load her with reproaches that fell with scanty grace
From lips of those who uttered them—the hypocrites,
　　the base.

What wonder that she met them with the scorn they
    well deserved?

Were they so fully righteous? Had they never weakly
    swerved

From the narrow path of honour, that they spoke such
    taunts to her,—

She, who knew them, knew their actions which not
    any dare aver—?

But they silenced her with roughness such as only
    man would use,

With the coarsest taunts and censure, her yet hard'ning
    heart to bruise,

As they led her to the Temple, in her mask of bitter
    scorn,

To defile its sacred precincts with their oaths so
    foully sworn.

She entered boldly, proudly, 'spite the sinking of her
    heart,

Where a mingling of emotions surged with many a
    new-felt smart.

The surroundings of the Temple had recalled the
    lovely dream

Of those fairest hours of childhood, ere the troubled,
    muddy stream

Of temptations never conquered soiled the current
    of her days,

And the shadow of transgression dimmed the bright-
    ness of Love's rays,

For the annals of her girlhood had been fair and pure,
    as Love

Makes of life the best and purest when admitted from
    Above—

But she cast aside these heart throes, and upheld her
    worn, proud head,

Stepped between the Temple portals with a firm and
    noiseless tread,

Mocking with her faded beauty those real charms that
    once had been,

As the stormy shades of Winter mock the Summer's
    brilliant sheen.

Her accusers faced the Master, and she too upraised
    her eyes,

Meeting His, so full of knowledge, yet in sweet
    compassion's guise ;

And a flush of shame and sorrow swept the scorn
    from all her brow,

Shook the pride from her demeanour, led her bur-
    dened soul to bow

In repentance, in contrition at the feet of mercy's King,

To pour out her mute confession with its inner
    self-made sting.

Her accusers told their story ; true, though ill of grace
    in them,

As they waited, eager, ruthless, for the Master to
    condemn ;

Waited, yet in vain expectance, lingered but to hear
    returned

Stern reproach for their accusings, inner heart intents
    discerned.

" He among you who is faultless," spake the Master's
    true clear tones,

" Shall by right of his own virtue, cast the first death-
wingéd stones !"
In the shame of deep conviction crept they forward,
one by one,
Till th' accused was with the Master left in penitence
alone,
Left with her awakened conscience to receive her due
reward,
Left to know her soul's Redeemer, earth's one Judge
and Heaven's Lord.
" Woman, where are thine accusers?" spake the
ringing Voice again ;
" Was there no one to condemn thee?" and, in
whispered words of pain,
She replied with anguished sobbings, those the flood-
gates of new grief ;
" No man, Lord".........And lo, the Master, ever
swift to grant relief,
Answered gently, with forgiveness pent in every glance
He bore,
"Neither then do I condemn thee; go thy way, and
sin no more."
Wondrous grace of boundless mercy ! in thy full free
overflow
Poetry, the life of genius, had its further dower
below,
To mature its growing beauty, to prepare the buds of
Spring
For the fuller growth the Summer of accomplishment
should bring.

—————:o:—————

At the base of Olive's mountain as the shades of
    evening closed,
When the ceasing of the daylight in sweet peace and
    rest reposed,
O'er the flowing brook of Kidron went they forth,
    a gentle band,
With the echoes of their evening hymn still whisp'ring
    through the land.
To the Garden of Gethsemane they trode the quiet way,
Where the calm of Nature's solitude had marked the
    twilight grey,
Where the still leaves drooped in silence, and the
    dewy-laden flowers
Hung their brilliant heads lamenting for the noontide's
    brighter hours.
There the weary travellers halted; the disciples to
    find rest
In the old and lovely garden, which of all they loved
    the best;
There they sat in quiet converse,—all but One who
    toiled in prayer—,
Till deep slumber took them gently to its fancy-
    curtained snare;
And they slept, the weary resting, every sorrow cast
    aside;
They had peace: but *He*, their Master, Brother,
    Friend, and constant Guide,
Toiled in agonized petitions born of sorrows long and
    deep;
He was weary past all knowledge, yet had but to pray
    and weep.

Why? Because His Love was winning yet another
  glorious fight;
And because that Love was victor, so He toiled the
  long, dark night,
Till the dawn of morning found Him conqueror,
  though doomed to die,
Found Him in the Hall of Judgment—pale His face,
  but calm His eye—
Lonely, and in noble silence; but not thus His
  suffering less,
Still a type of pain-wrung manhood, though Divine in
  righteousness;
Standing there, a King derided, and unflinching in
  the broil
Of a thousand mocking voices in their fierce insane
  turmoil.
Now, a pause; as Pontius Pilate nervously proscribes
  his peace,
Giving to a murd'rous robber an unmerited release,
Doing, with his *passive* judgments, an injustice and a
  crime,
Scarcely equalled in the records of the history of all
  Time,
To a son of spotless manhood, to the only type on
  earth
Of the highest in all virtue, honour, love, and mental
  worth.

Yet another scene of sorrow, and the darkest ever
  known;

On the Cross a King is dying, in His self-sought death
 alone,
With the heavy crushing burden of a world's dark
 sins to bear,
And no light divine of Heavenly love His lonely grief
 to share ;
With no aid nor hope to sweeten the cup of woe He
 drinks
In that moment of long agony the human spirit shrinks,
And trembles at the darkness of the sins it bears away
Into the deep oblivion of a never reckoned day.
Oh ! those pangs of awful anguish, human only in
 their pain,
Far above all common sorrows in their spirit-rending
 strain,
And Divine in their accomplishment, soul-victory over
 death,
Transcendant in the mighty Peace made ours with
 every breath !
The darkness grows more potent, the Cross is lost in
 gloom,
As the Soul of earth's one Saviour stoops to meet her
 threatened doom ;
One thrill of fearful agony that shakes a frightened
 world,
One stifled moan of anguish, and the load of sin is
 hurled
Far below th' abyss engulfing thought of memory's
 stern school,
Far beyond the yawning chasm where bold death
 holds gruesome rule,

Far beyond, and ever further from the rays of earth's
    fair light,
To th' unfathomable chaos of the darkest, deepest
    night.
Swiftly from the bounds of darkness comes the Spirit
    back to Heaven;
One last whisper: "It is finished!" and a doomed
    world is forgiven
Through the glorious atonement of a dying Saviour's
    blood;
Man made one with his Redeemer in unceasing
    Brotherhood;
Christ th' Incarnate Lord surrendered at the sacrificial
    shrine,
Man, the guilty, fallen, dying,—saved by might of
    Love Divine.

———:o:———

Laud it over all the ages as the theme of fairest praise;
This the boundless Love inspiring every Poet's highest
    lays;
This the Love, itself a poem sweet and tender, true
    and strong,
Which alone is the Eternal Inspiration of all song!

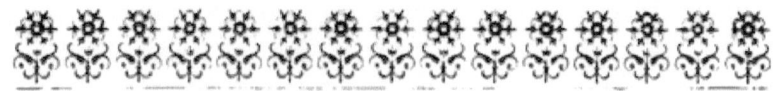

Nature's Sympathy.

THE world is beautiful!
And with a beauty that can change
To suit our every mood,
As if it understood
Our vagaries, so fleeting and so strange;
As if the green-clad trees,
Their branches swaying in the summer breeze,
Were fitted for our life's most brilliant hours,
While chilly snow-laid fields, with gloomy skies,
Make Winter's first, chief prize,
Where in the death-cold gloom the sad heart cowers.

The innate sympathy
By every budding flower expressed,
In every cloud confined,
And whispered by the wind,
Is beautiful, and in its beauty blest.
The wood-bird's happy trills
Are but an echo of the joy which thrills
Our own glad hearts, in days of deepest peace,
And lonely, restless Ocean's heaving sobs
Blend with our own heart throbs,
Our grievous sighs and murm'rings for release.

The sunshine's radiance
Holds kinship with the love so bright,
    That cheers our onward way,
    And bids the clouds delay,
The clouds of fear which make our darkest night.
    So every bird that sings,
And every insect with his varied wings,
Have a sweet message given them to outroll;
Or with a silence that is deep content,
    Nature gives kind assent
To those great feelings which uplift the soul.

With the Flowing of the Tide.

WHERE the merry bright-hued ripples mark the
    flowing of the tide,
Where the sunshine o'er the ocean lingers fair in
    gracious pride,
Where the heavy-freighted vessels sail in majesty
    along,
Flows the burden of my song.

There beside the weed-laid margin of the smooth
    shell-spangled sand,
Where the murmur of the ocean echoes deep along
    the strand,
The resounding of the billows far across the spacious
    bay
Is refrained in ocean spray.

There the sea-breeze brought a message from the
    kingdoms of the west,
To a weary heart a message of eternal happy rest,
Which the stately, heaving ocean, in its boundless
    azure brings
On the morning's silver wings.

And a tired heart found comfort in the gently-sweet
    repose,
That only from the restlessness of the ocean-spirit
    flows ;
So the merry sun bathed ripples, dancing carelessly
    along,
Brought me peace to end my song.

The First Spring Flowers.

HALF-BLOWN wreaths of Laurestinus
    Blushing fair amid the green,
Nodding such a glad'ning welcome
    In their modest, graceful mien;
And they tell me Spring is coming,
    Spring is coming! Spring, my queen!

While the sweet white-robed Narcissus
    Gently waves his golden bells,
And the proudly-smiling floweret
    Still the same glad chorus swells;
Still the glad refrain is pealing:
    Spring is coming through the dells!

Sweetest heralds of the Springtide,
    With their songs of trust and hope,
How they still the moans despondent
    Of my heart where sorrows grope,
And there dawns a new, bright gladness,
    With its miseries to cope;

And the sunshine through the tree-tops
    Takes a fresh inspiring power;
While the passing of the daylight
    Bears this burden in each hour:
Spring is coming in its glory,
    With its wealth of bud, and flower!

Spring is coming with its promise
　　Of the fuller glories there,
When the brilliance of achievement
　　Shall adorn the Summer air,
And the measure of true beauty
　　Shall fulfil the promise fair.

Earth's Ever Changing Canopy.

AS changing and as beauteous as the sea
　　So vast, so buoyant, deep, and wildly free,
　The sky is still more fathomless and vast ;
Its often radiant, rainbow tinted hue,
Its frequent aspects of unrivalled blue,
　　All charm us with their beauty unsurpassed.

The brilliance of the sun's awakening beams,
The sky's deep purple lit with golden gleams
　As night's shade brightens into dazzling day ;
The startling splendour of the early dawn,
To our dim sight becomes a veil half-drawn
　A glimpse of ideal glories to display.

The fleecy clouds like wingéd angels fair
Constrain us still to breathe a humble prayer,
    To raise our souls towards Heaven's high Mercy-Seat ;
Uplifted from our weariness and pain,
Our song ascends, a glad and thankful strain,
    Far through the sky, earth's holy incense sweet.

The storm clouds which the lightning fierce reveals,
(Our awe increased by solemn thunder peals),
    Have fearful grandeur fraught with danger's gloom ;
And as the mighty echoes strike our ears,
Filling each heart with haunting unknown fears,
    The answering winds in mockery shriek our doom.

The beauty of the evening, calm and still,
The Sun's reflection, from the Western hill
    Spreading an orange glow across the blue,
Strangely enthrals our senses as we gaze
Until the glow is lost in twilight haze ;
    So rapidly it passes from our view.

But even Sunset, richly warm and bright,
Cannot excel the moon-lit clouds of night,
    When lovely Luna, consort of the Sun,
Looks earthward from her airy throne of state,
To gladden hearts that bend 'neath sorrow's weight,
    To cheer us when our daily tasks are done.

The Torn Portrait.

IT was sadly torn and injured
   Where destroying hands had lain;
All the wrappings of the figure
   Were as spent links of a chain;
And the ruined twisted fragments,
   Lying scattered all around,
Were belike the leaves of Autumn
   On the forest's verdured ground.

All the beauty of the features
   In their grace was marred and bent,
And the lip's fair bloom had faded
   As culled roses lose their scent;
Ev'n the forehead, with its power,
   Its clear signs of inward thought,
Lay a crushed and battered emblem
   Of what spoiling Time hath wrought.

But the eyes—? Ah, here the vandal
   Trembling failed, and incomplete
Left the work of his poor malice,
   Brooking only forced defeat;
And amid the scattered fragments
   Gleamed there forth with life-like fire,
Eyes to melt in sweetest pity,
   Eyes to flash with sudden ire.

Living orbs, wherein the Spirit
  Looks beyond its home of clay
Into life's great consummation,
  Dawning in Eternal Day.
There they rest, those painted mirrors
  Where the soul was pencilled deep,
Truly showing each expression
  Into which life's light may creep ;

There reflecting, what the Spirit
  Else must veil in silence long,
Shadowing, in misty colours,
  Purple depths of feeling strong,
Writing, in strange hieroglyphics,
  Traces of the heart's long strife,
Giving to the true receiver
  All the outlines of a life.

So they lay, unshattered symbols
  Of the soul they shadow forth,
(As the clear sun of the midnight,
  In the deep sky of the North,
Is an emblem, fair and brilliant,
  Of the same which gives our day)
And the symbols of the Spirit
  In its clothing of frail clay,

Are as lasting, as triumphant
  Over death's destroying power ;
When the Soul shall find its future
  After dissolution's hour,

When the shadows of death's valley
  Roll beyond the brilliant heights
Of the Life that Soul shall welcome,
  As it ends its wayward flights.

It shall live, this lonely Spirit,
  Wearied now with prison bars;
It shall gain its best existence,
  Freed from all these bondage scars;
It shall live of Life the highest
  In fair liberty's domain,
Where the shades of sin and sorrow
  Never cast the whitest stain.

It shall live, and in its living
  Cease to know the bonds once worn;
Liberty! Where ev'n memory
  Fails to bring a Past we mourn.
In the life of only pureness
  All unrighteousness must flee,
When the Soul, enslaved no longer,
  Lives in grandest Verity.

A Picture.

A belt of sky, a strip of sea,
    The blue waves rolling wild and free,
Foam crested billows tossing high;
A fair expanse of sea and sky.

The azure margin of the strand
Contrasting with its shining sand
And forming one fair harmony,
The pœan of the flowing sea.

One shaded, shimmering, drifting cloud
Hov'ring above, a spirits shroud;
The spirit of a Summer's dream
Floating across Time's sunlit stream.

The snowy wing-spread seagulls rest,
The sunbeams glancing o'er each breast,
Midway between the sky and shore,
The plumaged guards of aerial store.

*   *   *   *

A Picture? Nay; a poet's song,
    An inspiration of the soul,
The whisper of the laureate throng,
    The echo of a minstrel's dole.

A picture? Yes; the fairest art
  That blent a poem in each wave,
That speaks rare gifts to every heart,
  And hides itself in what it gave.

A picture? Yes; an earth-born child,
  But bearing Nature's stamp alone,
And as she sweetly danced and smiled,
  The artist made her grace his own.

A picture? Yes; a living sweep
  Of hallowed sky and throbbing sea,
The noblest rendering of the deep,
  A bright inspiring symphony.

The Face of Love.

BEFORE me in the shadows of a dream
   I see one face outlined, a sweet young face,
Resplendent, glowing with the fairest grace
   In which the deep lights of the pure soul gleam.
There where the shadows cast their misty veils
O'er the far past, where even memory fails,
Where scarce one ray may shed its dim, faint beam,
I see it in the shadows of a dream :
      That one pure Spirit-face.

I have no written word, nor short nor long,
Of what those tender lips might once express,
I have no memory ev'n of one caress,
   Nor one brief echo of a sweetest song ;
Only I know, I feel it in my heart,
Where every reason fails to take its part,
I know that in that face, so pure, so strong,
One message only bore its charm along :
      The charm of perfect Love.

And in the dear dream face I see it still :
The Love that lives through all the lapse of years,
The Love that conquers legion doubts and fears,
   And bravely bears itself through every ill.
In shadows I must see it now, but soon,
When draws to night life's present afternoon,
And night to endless day, that Love shal fill
My soul with satisfying joy, until
      I too shall learn to love.

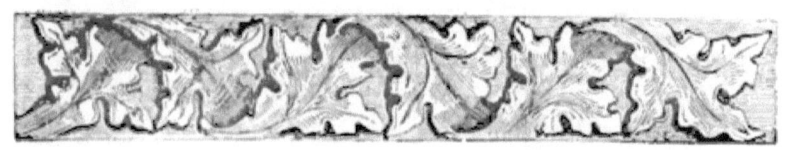

Buttercups.

I saw some golden buttercups,
    And they grew in a London field,
When the grass was rank, and their stems were lank,
    But their beauty was unconcealed,
    As a fair emblazoned shield.

I saw some golden buttercups;
    They were clasped by a childish hand,
And a face was bright with a happy light,
    As if caught from the glory-land,
    Where the white-robed angels stand.

I saw some golden buttercups,
    Where they bloomed on a turf-laid wall;
And each yellow head to the sun was spread,
    Whose bright rays shone over them all,
    I noted the glad beams fall.

I saw some golden buttercups;
    They were crushed in an old cracked jar,
But they lit the gloom of a dreary room,
    Like the gleam of a heavenly star
    Thrown down from its seat afar.

I saw some golden buttercups,
Which were sketched with an artist's skill;
In each fair wee flower was its brilliant dower,
Confined by the sheeny frill;
And their beauty lingers still.

Whene'er I view the buttercups,
With their wonderful golden sheen;
It just seems to me that there may not be
A lovelier sight to be seen,
In the empires of the green.

The Song of Faith.

THE morning dawned with a dismal chill,
    The sky was heaped with its clouds of grey
The mists crept over the field-laid hill,
    Dark'ning the promise of perfect day;
The cold wind shivered about the trees,
    Scathingly biting the new-formed leaf;
The clouds rolled on till they met the seas,
    And stranded on the horizon reef.

The dawn was dull, and my heart was sad,
   Till a wee bird flew to my window pane,
A songster, not of the brightest clad,
   But trilling songs of the sweetest strain.
The clouds passed on in forebodings deep,
   And the bird still warbled his joyous lays;
The fears in my heart were lulled to sleep
   By th' echoes there of that song of praise.

I watched the hill with its misty dress,
   I scanned the grey of the dull, dark sky,
I felt the breeze's enchilled caress,
   But over all was that joyful cry;
And I knew that noon would be fair and bright,
   I trusted still in the God-given song,
And waited there for the pure sunlight
   To gleam when the clouds had swept along.

In hope I watched till the gloom had passed,
   Till the breeze had taken a warmer drift,
Till the sun shone fair o'er the hill at last,
   And gaily scattered his morning gift;
And amid the beams of the glowing sun,
   Chasing the mist to the valley's close,
My Faith increased in the hope begun,
   And doubts lay wrapt in their noon repose.

The Flower Star of Spring.

OH, why do they call thee the emblem of sadness,
　　Pale, sweet, modest primrose, ah, canst thou
　　　　say why?
When our eager glance rests on thy fair soothing beauty,
And we willingly gather thy morsels of fragrance,
Is aught in that beauty to sadden the eye,
Or cast down our spirits, or call forth a sigh?

No, not when we plucked thee, as free and light-hearted
We joyously rambled through woodland and dell;
Quite content to exist in the joy of the moment,
All enrapt with our simple discernment of Nature,
Uncritical, pleasing.　Heigho! we know well
The pleasures of childhood we grasped ere they fell.

Is part of thy mission, fair primrose, beloved,
To bring to remembrance the days of lost youth?
Oh, is this the lone cause of the mist o'er our vision,
And the tear trembling over the sad drooping eyelash?
Aye, utter it softly, but whisper the truth,
If grace may incline to a thing so uncouth.

But, blossom, we miss now the pride of thy beauty;
As resting in state on the däis of green,
Thou hast budded and bloomed in thy fair woodland
    palace,
While distributing gifts in a measure unbounded;
Sweet miniature sovereign, thy kingdom, we ween,
Is spacious to boast such a shy little queen.

To-day we admire, although in thy dominion
To trace willing footsteps falls not to our share;
It may be that we traverse the streets of a city,
'Mid the whirl of its turmoil and business-bound
    pressure,
And read thy sweet message displayed even there;
What wonder, that reading, a sigh moves the air?

The sadness is transient, a fleeting emotion,
But not the less truly a genuine regret;
Those the brightest and best of the days of our spring-
    time,
With the years are now passing for once and for ever;
Ah! Primrose, their memory we would not forget,
And thus for remembrance, fair flow'r, we have met.

Newquay.

NEWQUAY, Bride of Northern Cornwall,
   Plighted by the grand old sea,
With the music of the breakers
For a full and glorious anthem ;
   And the Heaven's wide canopy,
To supply the dimmer arches
   Of our lesser, sculptured fanes ;
While the low voice of the breezes,
   With its soft, subduing strains,
   Give a choir's rich refrains.

As a maiden for her bridal
   Is bedecked with robe and band,
So our Newquay wears a garment—
Crossed by many a rocky girdle,—
   Of the sweeping, shining sand ;
And a veil of misty splendour
   Morn and Even give the bride ;
While the showers of wedding favours
   Are the treasures of the tide,
   Scattered round on every side.

Can we give a greater blessing
   To our favourite of the shore,
Than already she possesses
In her ocean-bound dominion?
   We can grant her nothing more
Than our full and free affection;
   Just the bond we vassals pay
To our royal, noble lady,
   And her liege, the warrior grey,
   Of our land the rocky stay.

Morning Sunshine.

GLORIOUS, ever-welcome sunshine
   Brightening all the morning hours,
Sunshine gladdening all the meadows,
   Sunbeams dancing o'er the flowers,
Gleaming through the budding tree-tops,
   Sparkling on the dew-moist lawn,
Sketching fair in glowing colours
   All the beauties of the dawn.

Fairest gleams of fairest brilliance
  Shining through each rifted cloud ;
Sweetest arrows tipped with radiance
  Darting o'er the still night's shroud ;
Heralds bright in gold and silver,
  Heralds of the gladsome day,
Dawning in its purest robing,
  Clad in simple, sweet array.

Merry, merry dancing sunbeams !
  Happy, happy rays of hope !
Bringing gladness o'er the hillside,
  Scattering jewels down the slope ;
Chanting silent songs of pleasure,
  Breathing joy's supreme delight ;
Welcome ! Glad and happy sunshine,
  Fully welcome, gladly bright.

Lent Lilies.

THE yellow heads toss in the wind ;
  The golden bells glisten with dew ;
Come love, we will gather the daffodils sweet,
  And the best shall be, Baby, for you.

The fairest and best we can seek,
  To match with each bright, golden lock,
To vie with the loveliest blossom of all
  That across the green meadowland rock.

The daffodils, lilies of Lent,
  Betoken regard, the folks say,
And so I will pluck a big posy of love
  To deliver my message to-day.

The yellow heads toss in the wind,
  And play with wild March's rough breeze,
All nodding and shaking in frolicsome glee,
  As if seeking the sun to displease.

Their antics are merry and gay,
  Their beauty a brilliant delight,
But after all, dearest, what else can compare
  With her baby to mother's fond sight ?

My Lent Lily, darling, are you ;
  You came, in the Spring's early hours,
To gladden the garden of Mother's own love
  With the fairest of all the bright flowers.

The daffodils, baby, are sweet ;
  You love them, and so, dear, do I ;
But one little flow'ret I love, oh far more
  Than all others beneath the blue sky.

Among the Primrose Gatherers.

WITH loud merry laughter and shrill happy song
    The children go joyfully dancing along,
While the fatherly sun his warm rays o'er them sheds,
On their bright careless faces, and rough tangled heads.

Through lanes and green meadows they wander at will,
Their hands always busy, their feet never still;
And the old battered baskets, so dirty and frail,
Grow resplendent and fragrant with primroses pale.

One lithe handsome youngster, decked gaily with fern
And golden-eyed blossom, no artist could spurn,
For the lad makes a picture of pure healthy glee
That the older heart longs in its seared bloom to see.

Then joyously tripping beside this gay youth
Is a maiden in whose azure eyes we read truth;
And there rests a stray lock of her long golden hair
'Mong her flowers, and lingers so radiant there.

Two babies are playing across the soft grass;
And, guarded from harm by a motherly lass,
They are tumbling and rolling their dear tiny selves,
Without trouble or hurt, the wee mischievous elves.

It is such a fair scene with th' children and flowers
So freely enjoying the short, blissful hours,
That I long for the talent to faithfully trace
An immutable sketch of its beauty and grace.

But little feet tire, and the baskets are filled,
The sun sinks away, tiny fingers grow chilled;
And at last I am left in the dim silent lane
In the twilight, to ponder alone once again.

It ever is thus in our changeable world;
The sails of existence so swiftly are furled.
All our pleasures soon cease, and our sorrows are brief,
We are weary; Death's night brings us rest and relief.

Fancies.

WE close our eyes to beauty,
    And say to ourselves with a sigh :
Our life has no brightness, no pleasure;
    We only are left to die.

We people earth with phantoms,
    The spirits of doubt and of fear,
And groan in our weakness and blindness :
    No comforting faith is here.

We clothe each hour with shadows
   Of sorrow, and desolate care,
And murmur : Existence is dreary,
   A desert where joy is rare.

We bow our heads in sickness,
   And whisper with fluttering breath :
We are tired of life and its conflict,
   And long for thy call, O Death.

We fill the air with fancies,
   Till the day grows as dark as night ;
But one breath of God's happy favour
   Turns gloom into gladdest light.

The dreams are grim and fearsome,
   And the fanciful hides the true ;
But their antidote is in loving faith,
   And the will and power to do ;

To do the good that's nearest
   With a trusting and kindly heart,
Till the gloomy clouds of our dreary lives
   In cheeriness drift apart.

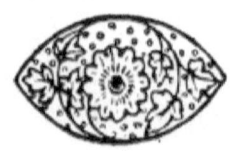

The Hawthorn.

FAIR Hawthorn and Hope! the words go together,
    Speaking of joy and the warm sunny weather.
How blithely we welcome this flower of the May,
Transforming the earth with apparel so gay;
The gleam of its petals all shimmering white,
Its fair lovely foliage, so green and so bright,
The scent of its perfume—all tell us again,
While the breeze in its boughs sings the same sweet
    strain :
The Spring is among us! In splendour appearing,
Its wonders are ours, and the Summer is nearing.

Fair Hawthorn and Hope, sweet symbols of gladness;
Aye, vanish all grief and sorrow and sadness!
The lovely May-blossom is shining around,
A message from Heaven where e'er it is found.
Impassive, unclosed, through the evening's dim hours,
Spread out to the sky are its pale, graceful flowers;
Awaiting in hope till the night-curtains, drawn
By the clouds, shall open to welcome the dawn;
Expecting, in confidence, daylight's approaching,
And greeting the sun o'er the hill-side encroaching.

Hawthorn, the Springtide's particular glory,
Shed o'er all meadowland, telling her story ;—
The tale of how Winterdom drew to its close,
And how her own empire with majesty rose ;
Revealing in beauty the dreams of a seer,
Foretelling the Summer-green soon to appear ;
Hawthorn, the minstrel and prophet of Spring,
The pride of all Nature, the work of a King,
Its wonderful blossoms we joy in displaying,
And give ourselves up to the pleasures of Maying !

The Convict's Baby.

" **H**E'S dying ! " then shortly they add, " He is
dead ! "
But never a tear o'er the still form is shed.
And why ? It were folly to grieve at his gain,
The poor child who had borne such a life of pain ;
And well do they know it, those folks we term hard,
As they calmly discuss " the poor little card."

Yes, dead ! Of neglect and starvation he died,
For want of the care which we *Christians* denied
" We never refused !" do I hear all around?
No ; we only pass heedless where sorrows abound,
Reproaching the poor who lack leisure to weep
O'er the baby who rests in his last sweet sleep.

But wan faces light up as the words pass on :
" He died of starvation, the baby has gone !"
Bleared eyes grow more fiery, rough tones become
    loud,
Till it ends in an angry, riotous crowd,
All fiercely demanding redress of their wrongs,
Asserting the right which to England belongs.

There are cries of " A riot !" Policemen march out,
And speedily put the insurgents to rout.
The leaders are led to the gaol, one by one,
A result of the death of the factory-girl's son ;
The police do their duty, receive their reward,
But ah, can that baby's frail life be restored?

His father ? A felon of noted ill-fame ;
Yet should the child starve for his parent's bad
    name ?
His mother is only a convict's young wife,
Who once helped her husband to save his weak life
An " accomplice " finds work so hard to procure,
To live is a struggle, and just means endure.

So th' baby was starved, while our guardians stand by
And proclaim that the workhouse is always nigh.
That wife was a mother with fond, loving heart,
Who felt that she could not so readily part
With her only child. But alas! for her grief,
Her babe has now passed beyond earthly relief.

She was willing to toil, and did her work well,
But her wage was a fraud, her work-room a hell;
The girl wife and mother was honest and brave,
Yet the baby now lies in a starveling's grave;
She carries a grief-stricken heart in her breast,
But her toil must go on without change, without rest.

The sigh of that mother, the wail of her boy,
Shall mingle for ever with anthems of joy.
May they reach every heart, that we all may hear,
From the tradesman's lad to the cynical peer,
That desolate sigh, and the starving child's moan,
As they blend with the rioters' sullen groan;

Till all, moved by pity and love, are impelled
To stop the oppression and tyranny held
Over workmen by masters, by rich over poor,
To grant bread to the wee hungry babes who implore
By their weak, feeble cries, the succour and aid
Of every true parent the Father hath made.

I will give thee the treasures of darkness. (Isaiah xlv, 3).

Thou hast set my feet in a large room. (Psalm xxxi, 8).

THE weary shadows press; the deepening gloom
   O'erhanging all, subdues my inmost sense;
And in the darkness of my soul's close room,
Where in the shade I read an awful doom,
   My spirit falters in the twilight dense;
There in deep cloud I stumble, vainly grope,
Yet of myself may find no cord of Faith, no light of
     Hope.

Only of God is light. He sends to me
   The faith I need, and faith brings hopeful trust;
And from the darkness is my spirit free,
Loosed from the bonds of sin, and hell's decree,
   Which bound me down, a slave to tyrant dust
Of doubt, despair and all-despondent sin.
Thank God! He sent me loving faith, and hope-light
     flooded in.

And from the darkness of my gloomy soul
  Rich, heavenly treasures have been brought to light.
He set them there, who made my spirit's whole;
He set them deep, below the angry roll
  Of sinful passions in my nature's night ;
And now, in His Own time, He calls them out—
The treasures of His Love, set there beyond all sin
    and doubt.

So where His light reveals the inmost deep
  Of this my soul, I find it close no more ;
For only where doubt's darkest shadows creep,
And only where sin's dust piles many a heap,
  Can aught confine the spirit's threshing-floor ;
So where God's light of Love dispels all gloom,
My soul has rest where He has set me in His Own
    "large room."

Wild Flowers.

A splendid bouquet of wild treasures they brought
    me,
  Fresh and sweet from the hedgerow, the marsh,
    and the brake,
Which lavish such fragrance and splendour around me
  'That I cannot but love them for fair Beauty's sake.

Osmunda ! Thou king of all ferns, celebrated
  And long-honoured by minstrel in ballad and rhyme;
How welcome thy shade near the cool, rippling
    streamlet,
  'Neath the tall leafy trees in the warm summer time !

Not less art thou welcome 'mid Orchis and Iris,
  Brilliant blossoms, thy emerald beauty to grace ;
And with more of thy kin, though none like thee so
    royal,
  Is the tall stately Fox-glove in dignity's place.

Fair starred Marguerita and sweet Honey-suckle
  Nestle closely together in mutual bliss,
And the frail Briar-roses with pure perfumed petals,
  To my fancy seem fit for an angel's soft kiss.

Yet far more do I love them, th' sweet silent flow'rets,
  For the message of patience and love which they
    bear,
A God-given example of trust in His mercy,
  A full proof that our Father for all things doth care.

A Song of Love.

LOVE is the key of richest treasure,
    Unlocking youth's fair house of pleasure,
  The gem which brightens every dream,
  The sunlight of life's flowing stream,
The heaping of every measure.

Ah, love is fair and love is golden;
The ever new and the grandly olden!
  Love is a kingdom's jewelled crown,
  A prince's couch of the softest down,
Where rest is never with-holden.

Love is a song of Angel's chanting,
Our brightest hopes in nothing daunting;
  For love we dare our valour's best,
  Nor ever dream of award less blest
Than love which is ever haunting.

Love is the great Eternal Dawning,
When Earth's deep shades shall yield to morning,
  The fears of sin and doubt be past,
  And loving faith gleam fair at last,
All lesser love-beams scorning.

The Child-heart within us.

THE child-heart within us
    Prompts the happy, merry smile,
As the moments to beguile,
   We have lingered with the children,
And have joined their hearty glee,
With a zest so fully free,
   That our eager smiles and laughter
Chase some clouds of life away,
Till the children's happy play
   Holds for us the deepest plea.

   The child-heart within us
Gives the gentle tears which flow,
As we hear the tale of woe
   From some half-forgotten school-friend,
Or the playmate of past years;
And these sympathetic tears
   Check the growing rise of chillness,
Of indifference in our lives,
And the warmer influence strives,
   Till sweet victory appears.

The child-heart within us
Is the rich and flowing source
Of our sympathy's deep force,
    And the smiles and tears of manhood
Are the outcome of that spring;
And its blessings hold no sting
    In their pure and healthful moisture,
Only drops of loving peace,
Such as ever may increase
    For the praise-cup of our King.

Forget-Me-Not.

THEY have sent me the sweetest flowerets seen,
    Some pink and blue starlets, a few sprigs of green;
And each has its whisper, a faint tiny plea,
Just made known in silence to you and to me.

Away from the wood where the wild flowers blow,
And missing the dell where all sweet blossoms grow;
This the first message my posy has spread :
" Forget not the charm of my old mossy bed."

With much patient waiting we yet may hear more,
The fairest remembrance of scenes passed before ;
In gardens of beauty we ramble again,
And away through the woods and the dear old green
    lane.

In dreams 'neath the trees of the orchard we sit,
And mark the bright splendour the warm sun has lit;
Or slowly we pause in the soft moonlight fair,
And gather a few of the small florets there.

With every new fancy the souvenirs sigh :—
" Ah, never let aught of such sweet memories die,
But keep them for ever locked close in your breast,
And the treasures will prove to be doubly blest.

" The world will seem hard if the heart shall grow cold,
Its pleasures and joys turn to bitters untold ;
Prize youth's cheery gladness and make it your own,
Life's harvest shall treble the pleasure thus sown.

" Keep every bright memory of days long ago ;
A token, however unmeaning or slow,
May tender you comfort on some future day
And chase a few moments of sorrow away.

" And th' sadder remembrance of soul-sickness past,
Must live with the rest in Life's treasure-house vast ;
Though you often may ponder why this should live on,
To grieve your poor heart for the years that are gone ;

" But oh, though so sad, it has reason to be,
The tide of those griefs flows towards the great sea,
And the memory, deterrent, leads many a soul
In darkness, in safety, to Life's final goal ! "

Our Sweet English Rhine--The Fal.

O lovely Fal, whose wooded banks
  To thy fair self give wondrous grace,
Of thee, loved stream, I fain would speak,
  And having power thy path would trace
As flowing onward, day by day,
Gently thou glideth on thy way.

Thou, changing ever, yet the same
  To me, whose memory loves to rove
Along thy winding silvery course ;
  Around thy path I oft have wove
Sweet thoughts of pleasures past and gone,
When love's fair sunlight o'er me shone.

As I, in frail and simple craft,
  Down on thy heaving breast did glide,
In the glad transport of those hours
  I dreamt not of what might betide,
I had no thought for care or grief,
Or that Life's joys would be but brief;

But those were days that now are past,
  Though ling'ring in my memory yet ;
Sweet joyous hours of honeyed bliss
  That could I, I would ne'er forget,
For they are graven on my heart
And in my dreams still bear a part.

E

List ! gentle river, to my song,
    And bear it onward toward the sea,
Accept the tribute I would bring,
    The meed of praise I grant to thee ;
Flow on, O Fal, with this refrain,
Ye rippling waves, take up the strain.

Reflected Light.

T HE birds flew out from the waving trees
    Up to the blue of the peaceful sky,
Soared in the drifts of a south borne breeze
    Under the gleam of the sun's bright eye,
Over the hills with their robes of green
    Trimmed with the softest red of the plough,
Into the heights of expanse serene,
    Beneath the snow of a cloudlet's brow.

The wind sang on in its woodland haunt,
    The whispered tales of the forest swept
Like the soft refrain of an evening chaunt,
    Over the mead where the willows wept.
All Nature's treasures displayed her best,
    Beneath the veil of a modest grace,
'To woo one's soul to an earthly rest,
    To loose the spurs of life's eager race ;

But th' birds continued their eager flight
   Up to the wreath of the nearest cloud,
Bathing their wings in the sunbeam's light,
   Shrined in the glory the sun avowed ;
And the glowing sheen of its glory rare
   Was borne to me by those dazzling wings,
As always the glow of brilliance fair
   Must be th' reward which such seeking brings.

I could not see, from my shaded seat,
   The radiant source of the reflex beams,
And so the birds from their high retreat
   Diffused the gift of those joyous gleams.
They winged their flight, but the joy they won
   Was not theirs only to spend or keep,
They gained the light of the high fair sun
   To share with me, in true service deep.

The soarers too, in the field of life,
   May wing their flight with a ceaseless toil,
And wrestle long with the earthly strife
   Our nature winds as a lengthy coil
About the path of the restless wings,
   Longing to rise to a purer height,
When the darker dust of a sin-world clings
   To turn the soul from its destined flight ;

But coils once rent, and the earth-mould lost,
   As the old time chain of a freed-man's past,
The soul may rise though at earnest cost,
   Up to the sunshine of life at last,

Above the whirl of unsettled din
　　Into the peace of expansive thought,
Beyond the mesh of the tyrant sin
　　Into the joy of a victory wrought ;

And th' sunshine gained of life's purer sky
　　In plenitude may be cast below,
To shed some joy where the shadows lie
　　Deep in the kingdom of sin and woe.
The peace and joy that have thus been reached
　　Must live to scatter their beams again,
As an old world maxim often preached
　　Starts into some thought of the newest strain.

No man may live to his higher needs,
　　Retrieve the ills of our Parents' Fall,
Without achieving the creed of creeds,
　　The truest lesson of Life for all ;
He learns in rising of Wisdom's best,
　　The purest life and the strongest love,
And the world receives as his last bequest
　　A fuller gleam of the Life above.

The Murder of Cleitus.

THE gorgeous hall of feasting is bedecked in good
    array ;
The rich and heavy curtains relegate the light of day ;
A full and varied banquet overlays the mighty board,
Till every dish is raided by the hearty practised horde.
The company is various, and numerous as great,
The king, his lords and warriors, the people of the
    state,

And Alexander heads the board with sumptuous,
    royal grace,
But foolish words are on his lips, the wine-flush on
    his face.
No victor is the monarch as he drinks the fiery wine,
Debased by weakest passions, he makes merriment
    for swine ;
He jests in mocking anger, or, convulsed with demon
    glee,
He shouts his loudest battle song in liquor minstrelsy.

The strife and noise grow wilder, hot ambition starts
    aflame
Burning with raging eagerness to prove its own dear
    fame.
The rival merits of the gods, the claims of jealous man
Make the conflicting elements in each discursive plan ;
And Cleitus roused vehemently, defies his monarch's
    word,
Defies it at the gleaming point of out-stretched,
    unsheathed sword.

They part the angry combatants, and Cleitus steps aside,
And with a touch of pained regard convicting greater
    pride,
He says in gentlest reference to Granica's dark fray :
" 'Twas this hand, Alexander, that preserved thee on
    that day."
But his sovereign scorns the soft reproof shot from
    those noble eyes,
And murmurs scathing, taunting words in whispered,
    secret guise ;

And Cleitus hears the whispers, and he notes the
    scornful voice ;
His blood is raised to fiercest wrath ; he makes no
    lengthened choice ;
He turns and meets his monarch with a sternest,
    inmost hate,
And not a tithe of fixed disdain those burning orbs
    abate ;
He wastes no words of passion, all his weapons lie
    in rest ;
He stands in every dignity of heart and nature drest.

The reeling king arises in a transport of blind rage,
Excited further by that hate no drunken smiles assuage;
Excited to a maddening heat of uncontrolled desire,
He fiercely yields to vengeance in the violence of
his ire.
One thrust, a flash of sparkling steel, a last-expiring
breath,
And Cleitus lies in grim repose, the slave of silent
death.

Fame.

FAME! Man's supreme desire; yet what is Fame?
A strange uncertain light, whose fitful gleams
Shine on but few of Fortune's many sons,
A faint and feeble glimmer lighting up
The top-most peak of that great mount, Ambition.
Steep is the winding path, and rough, and long,
By which earth's sons may reach th' illumined height;
Though one may sometimes gain the lofty goal
By straighter, shorter ways, all others strive,
And often vainly struggle many a year,
Sometimes a weary lifetime, but to fall
At last into th' abyss of deep oblivion,
Or, deeper still, disgrace. And oft when reached,

What is this Fame which men pursue till death
Or imbecility may overtake them?
What does it prove but bright illusion's snare,
Among whose chilly shade lurks disappointment?
The glowing light whose radiance seemed a charm,
When noticed from within the humble vale
Of steady labour, unassuming toil,
Takes but a tawdry glare when seen aloft,
When the calm eye of him who won its gifts
Can analyse, with all a critic's skill,
Its meanly kindled fire and glittering shams.
Delusive Fame! Ah, none enjoy o'ermuch
Of its unfrequent joys, for 'tis but scarce
Enjoyment that is granted to its slaves;
And foolish they who trifle with the peace
A humble busy life may give with gain,
Who spurn the joys they hold, with thoughtless strife
To struggle after mean, half-paltry Fame,
And in the struggle risk their earthly all.

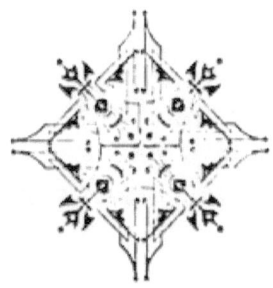

Summer's Dawn.

THE Spring of the year is passing,
   With its promise fair and sweet,
To be soon fulfilled, or blighted,
   In the blaze of Summer's heat ;
And the Spring of youth is speeding
   To the dawn of manhood near,
The Summer of life with its fuller blooms,
   The crown of existence here.

The Summer is crowned with flowers,
   And we would adorn thy days
With the best of Life's sweet blossoms
   To gladden the Future's ways ;
In affection's smoothest meadow,
   By the rippling brook of Love,
We would have thee walk, 'neath the holy light
   Of the smile of One above.

Manhood.

OH, be a man, my brother,
　　A man in deed and truth,
A noble 'mongst the noblest,
　　The Flower of flowery youth.
Strike out one line of action,
　　With effort true and strong;
Be earnest in its purpose,
　　And swerve not to a wrong.
Be steadfast in your life-work;
　　Aim high and work and wait;
'Tis not the idle dreamer
　　Shall o'erleap Fortune's gate.

To be a man, my brother,
　　Is not to hold a name
For honour, love and patience,
　　Yet undeserve its fame;
The youth wins fairest manhood,
　　Not when he gains its years,
But when he holds it stainless
　　Amid earth's fouler smears,
And when he counts his honour
　　Dearer than life or love,
Deeming all vices handled,
　　Crimes to his God above.

And such a man, my brother,
   Owns but a Father's hand
As Agent in his Future,
   Its import to command.
From God he takes all mercies,
   With thanks for Heavenly care ;
Gives with his cup of sorrow
   A strength-beseeching prayer.
He traces God's own power
   In records of the past,
And trusts alone in Jesus
   For peace while life shall last.

An English Landscape.

JUST a bit of lovely woodland,
   With a background of low hills ;
To the right the straggling village,
To the east a stretch of green sward
   Which the foreground also fills.

By the wood the little river
   Meekly winds its onward way,
Takes the mill stream in its running
Starts the several brooks with vigour,
   Winds its course toward the bay.

At the outskirts of the village
    Stands the ancient steepled church,
Half-concealed by verdant ivy,
And encircled with the linden,
    With the oak and silver birch.

On the hillside rests the manor,—
    Home of many an honoured squire,
Past and present—and its gables,
Fair and noble architecture,
    Mark fresh beauty in the shire.

Right before you is a farmhouse,
    With its garden, gay with flowers,
With its orchard and its dairy,
And the fields wherein the cattle
    Pass the summer's drowsy hours.

Just a rural English landscape,
    Have I pictured it aright?
Can you fancy all its details,
And its gentle, soothing beauty,
    Full of calm and sweet delight?

Just a country sketch from Britain,
    But to Englishmen more dear
Than all Jura's snowy summits,
Or Italia's ancient grandeur,
    Of dead hopes the mighty bier.

What are treasures oriental
    To the admired haunts at home?
What are France's brilliant vineyards,
Or the Fatherland's quaint cities
    Of the spire and the dome?

Even Norway's midnight splendour,
　Lofty mountains, deep-set lakes,
Rushing cascades, lonely canons,
Fall below our own loved standard
　That no loyal heart forsakes.

England's home-marked happy pictures
　Are enshrined in all our hearts;
Every son who calls her mother
Loves no other land the better,
　Never from his love departs.

The Unknown Song.

I heard a strange sweet sighing in the trees,
　　　　　　　　　And the breeze
It answered with a cadence low and long,
Like the softly dying echo of a song
　Borne afar across the quiet Summer seas.
The deep mysterious rhythm touched my heart
　With the gently healing spell of lovely peace,
And the spirit's rival conflicts fell apart
　Beneath the influence of this sweet increase.

The meaning of that song I did not know
       Long ago,
But a simple thought came to me in a dream,
On the fair unknown to cast a feeble gleam,
 A little spark from Wisdom's fuller glow.
The meaning of that song I still but guess,
And feel my thought is scanty to express
The deeper mystery of the holy chant
Whose very depth of meaning may but daunt
      My restless yearning, e'er returning,
To solve the problem of the song I hear,
So hard to understand, so sweetly clear.

 The secret is a knowledge from Above,
A little kindling, and from Heaven's own light,
 Borne on the wings of vision's silver dove,
And guided by its aid, serenely bright
      Amid the night
That ignorance had bound within my soul,
Again the soft, pure harmonies outroll,
 I hold their import in the one word, Love.

The Legend of the Carnations.

FAIR Lois of Flora's meynie
 Went tripping down the glade,
Tripping, skipping, skipping, tripping,
 Beneath the forest shade,
 As fair a lovely maid
 As any of the glade.

She reached to pluck a blossom,
 The sweet and wild dog-rose,
Swaying, playing, blithely swaying
 With every wind that blows,
 With every beam that glows,
 The fragrant briar rose.

She gently pulled the cluster,
 With pleased and smiling face,
Blushing, flushing, coyly blushing
 With shy and careless grace,
 A child of Ceres' race,
 With th' goddess' fair face.

But smiles gave way to sorrow,
    The face grew wet with tears ;
Sighing, crying, crying, sighing,
    Her fingers torn with spears,
    The thorns of rosy peers,
    Lois dewed her face with tears.

The blood-drops dyed the greensward,
    Rose-petals strewed the ground,
Glowing, blowing, sweetly glowing
    The green-clad earth around,
    As queenly Flora found
    In Cypra's forest-ground.

Fair Lois sat a weeping,
    But Flora bade her rise,—
Queenly standing, all-commanding—
    And dry her tear-moist eyes,
    To cease her childish sighs,
    And watch what might arise.

They gathered up the rose-leaves,
    And laid them in a wreath,
Sprinkled, wrinkled, blood-besprinkled,
    The red-dyed sward beneath,
    A grounding to bequeath
    The fragrant, tear-dewed wreath.

While yet the teardrops glistened,
    Queen Flora made few signs,
Telling, spelling, softly telling
    Some strangely mystic lines
    From magic fairy mines
    Of cabalistic signs.

The rose wreath, and the carmine,
  The tear-dews, gleaming bright,
Twining, shining, all combining,
  Soon disappeared from sight
  In blaze of sunny light,
  Magnificently bright.

The circle glowed with brilliance,
  The grasses bent aside,
Quaking, shaking, shaking, quaking,
  As if in shame to hide
  Their nodding heads of pride,
  A fairer grace beside.

The sweetest, little spikelets
  Of softest azured-green
Peeping, creeping, shyly peeping
  Above the ground were seen,
  Their new electric sheen
  A wondrous shade of green.

They grew, and bloomed in splendour ;
  The blossoms deeply red
Fading, shading, gently fading
  Into the whitest head ;
  Their intermedium spread
  With various tones of red.

The crimson held the blood-drops
  From Lois' fingers fair,
Glancing, dancing, dancing, glancing,
  Within the sunlight's glare,
  A blossoming as rare
  As Flora's beauty fair.

F

The palest were the tear-stained ;
　　The roses hid their scent,
Hiding, gliding, gliding, hiding
　　Among the petals bent,
　　At Flora's bidding pent
　　To yield their perfect scent.

The edge of every blossom
　　Was pinked to match the leaf
Coyly flirting, self-asserting,
　　Along the briary reef,
　　The cause of Lois' grief,
　　The rose's thorn and leaf.

The pretty, fragile spikelets
　　Were fashioned as the thorn,
Rasping, grasping, cruelly rasping,
　　Whence maiden-hands were torn
　　That sunny Summer morn ;
　　Oh ! naughty, harmful thorn !

Lois called her flowers *Carnations*
　　At Flora's sweet command,
Holding, folding, folding, holding
　　Still her wounded hand,
　　Whose deep-red scars yet stand,
　　The blossoms' long birth-brand.

Sailing.

SAILING on where the snowy foam
    Crests the blue of the rising waves,
Where the beat of the tide of home
    Echoes far from the deep-laid caves;
Sailing over the restless blue,
    Far away from dear England's strand;
Sailing fair with a noble crew
    Into the haunts of a distant land.

Sailing on to the shores unknown,
    'Set with many a danger snare,
Where the noise of the wind's dull moan
    Wanders over the storm-god's lair;
Sailing still with a calm, sure heart,
    Calm and sure till the voyage end,
Bravely taking the fiercest dart
    Winds may hurl, or the billows send.

Sailing on, so the true brave soul
    Calmly sails to the journey's close,
Undeterred by the surging roll,
    Undismayed by the greatest foes;
Sailing on, though the adverse fates
    Wrest the sails of her faith away;
Sailing still, while the harbour waits
    Past the surf and the wind-lashed spray.

Sailing on, and when life is fair,
  Holding still to her earnest toil,
Working yet for the night of care,
  Bravely 'quipped for a storm turmoil;
Sailing on, and when darkness falls,
  Shrouding the sky in sudden gloom,
Sailing straight 'mid the angry squalls
  That mark the track of th' thunder's boom.

Calmly on; so the soul's sure craft
  Sails secure to the end of life,
Not unharmed by the stormy shaft
  Flung from the bow of earthly strife;
Not unharmed, but to Peace at last
  The soul shall traverse life's short sea,
When storms shall sink in th' silent past
  That hides itself in Eternity.

Who shall separate?

BOWED in the darkness of silent grief,
    Torn with the conflict of inward strife,
Where is the joy of the Christian's life
In such pain as this, and such bitter woe?
Sad and weary our lot below;
    Never a helper and never relief?

Over the strife of the long commotion,
Over the waves of Life's heaving ocean,
Borne on the wings of a sorrow-wind,
Comes this message to all mankind :
Who shall separate, who shall sever
Us from the Love that is ours forever ?
Shall we lose it ? Ah, never, never !

The Love of Christ it is great indeed,
Mighty to vanquish a host of ills,
Gracious to render the Will of wills
The grand perfection of Right divine,
Where Justice, kneeling at Mercy's shrine,
In kindness succours our human need.

Purely true is the old world story
Telling in beauty and royal glory
The endless work of eternal Love
Resting beneath us, around, above ;
And nothing of Heaven nor earth shall sever
Our souls from th' Love that is conquered never,
The Love of Christ Who is King for ever !

Follow Me.

THOSE gentle words have caught our worldly ears,
   That loving smile has conquered all our fears,
And eagerly we hearken to His call
Spoken in tones which mystically enthrall
Our hearts, entrance our senses, as we see
His kindly face while speaking: " Follow Me!"

" Follow Thee, Lord? Yes, willingly," we cry,
" Ev'n unto death!" we haste to make reply,
And closely do we follow Him in peace;
We love to note His fame and power increase,
As patiently He goes from place to place
With loving, healing words and saving grace.

Joyously marching on the palm-strewn way,
We join th' hozanna and triumphal lay
Till mountains echo with the gladsome ring
That greets the son of David and our King;
Proud of our Leader, Lord and royal Friend,
Again we shout: " We'll serve Thee to the end!"

But oh! the time of darkness is at hand,
He told us, but we failed to understand.
He whispered of an awful troubled night,
Spoke of betrayal, and our shameful flight.
" Master!" we cried, "Not us? Ah Lord, not so,
Wherever Thou dost lead us we will go."

Yet now—Ah, let our heads be bowed with shame;
When that dark hour of trial and suffering came,
We went our ways, left Him to bear alone
The Cross, whose royal victim we to own
Even did shrink from.   Lord, wilt Thou forgive
Our dreadful shame of Thee, and let us live?

In seeking great things sadly have we failed,
For naught our loud professions have availed.
Contrite, repentant, we will humbly pray
Our gracious Lord to help us day by day.
Dear Master, grant us what we meekly ask,
Grace to fulfil the simplest daily task.

Our love is very weak, our service poor,
Yet, if we yield Thee all our earthly store,
Our wills, our faith, our loving service, all
We have to give, though these our gifts are small,
We know Thou in Thy mercy wilt receive
The lowliest we offer, who believe.

Again we hearken to that loving Voice
Bidding us follow still, but now our choice
Is not made blindly, for we know the way,
If we would follow Jesus every day,
Will not be easy, oft a dark rough road,
Yet still it is the pathway that He trode ;

And Christ is with us ! If we near abide
To our Redeemer, He will be our Guide,
And lead us safely to th' approaching end ;
God's guardian Angels too our steps attend,
They bear us upward, onward to the sky,
Still higher, to the Highest by and bye !

One Tenth for the Lord.

"ONE tenth for the Lord," so the Bible words read,
    "One tenth for the Lord," so the Parson had
       said,
But Meg, she was puzzled : What had she to give ?
An orphan with scarcely the wherewith to live,
And nothing in surety from which to afford
      One tenth to the Lord.

The youngest was Meg of a family of ten,
But several were dead, and the others grown men
With wives and wee babies to care for and feed,
Of their own tiny sister they took little heed,
And passed the commandment in God's Holy Word :
      One tenth to the Lord.

At last came the thought of what she might resign ;
Of brothers and sisters there once had been nine,
And she was the tenth ;—now would Jesus want more
Than her very own self, as she was so poor ?
Her life she would give Him, and thus would accord
      A tenth to the Lord.

But how could she offer herself as a gift ?
Ah, this was a problem whose troublesome drift
Was hard as the first one to rightly decide,
And many an hour Meg wearily tried
To learn how to give up herself to his ward,
      One tenth for the Lord.

Poor Meg wandered slowly along the great bridge,
Where, awkwardly perched on the cold stone-work
    ridge,
A playmate was sobbing o'er some childish grief;
Meg lingered, attempting a word of relief,
And plaintively told, until smiles were restored,
       Of th' tenth for the Lord.

A smile, and a movement, a splash and a cry !
Another, re-echoed, as Meg dashing by
Slipped over the coping, with frenzied intent
Of saving the mite, whose emphatic assent
Too gladly in boisterous eagerness poured,
       The tenth to the Lord.

The young child was saved while his fluttering breath
Still bravely defied the chill clutches of death ;
But Meg sank unaided beneath the cold wave,
Where th' deep-arched recess foiled all efforts to save,
Unheeded she passed from Life's busied record,
       A tenth for the Lord.

The rays of the moon o'er the city that night
Illumined the streets with a pale silvery light ;
They fell on the river, and caught the gold hair
Of the childish form floating so peacefully there ;
Poor Margaret had given in her love so assured
       Her tenth to the Lord.

Whither? What? When?

AH ! the restless, surging tide of Life,
　　Ah, whither doth it wend?
And the seeming ceaseless toil and strife,
　　Aye, will they ever end?
The blighted hopes, the weary sighs,
The pale sad cheeks, and tear-stained eyes,
The troubled moans, and anguished sighs ;
　　Say, where do all these tend?

And the current deep of mingled woe,
　　Is it not sea-ward bound,
To an endless deep where waters flow
　　Of misery profound—
Where joy and mirth are things unknown,
And song becomes a feeble moan,
Which soon resounds the hopeless groan
　　'Mid gallows' echoes found?

And the dreary years of grinding toil
　　Must surely cease some day ;
Might they not end in fierce turmoil,
　　If Death lead not the way?

When loosed shall be the pressing strain,
What shall soften those hearts again,
Which now grow hard in grief and pain,
    In sorrows grim and grey?

Alas for our race! But what can check
    The wild, relentless wave
That threatens all with a fatal wreck
    Far worse than th' bloodstained grave—?
The hardened heart, and defeated faith,
The poisoned truth of the coward's breath,
Ah! these are ills far worse than Death,
    A people to enslave.

Yet many their noblest years have lent,
    Taking a fixed bold stand
To kill the demon of discontent
    That spoils our native land;
Much is accomplished here and there
To ease th' oppressed of want and care,
But it is needful everywhere
    The good work to expand.

The task is great, and the work is long,
    And needing many a care
To plan the best, and to right the wrong
    In the depths of sin's dark lair;
Naught will kindle a ray of light
'Mid the clouds of the deepest night,
Naught but the power of Love's own might,
    The only power that dare.

Ah! When shall the rushing tide be turned
    From frenzy's rebel sea?
And when shall the castaways long spurned
    Be raised from misery?
When all men truly act their part,
And Love burns warm in every heart,
Then shall be healed the bitter smart
    Of woe-pressed slavery.

A Sketch.

A sheaf of golden lilies,
    The glowing asphodels,
Bound by an azure garland
    Of nodding fairy bells,
A childish face above them
    With sunlit golden hair,
And blue eyes brightly peeping
    Between their lashes fair;
A loving word of greeting,
    Cooed with a smiling grace,
And baby hides her dimpled charms
    In mother's fond embrace.

Life's Secret.

THEY were only the thought of a moment,
   And forgotten as soon as expressed
By the speaker, but carefully treasured
   In the listener's sorrowful breast;
Yet the words in themselves were quite simple,
   Just a soft " I'm so sorry, my dear,"
Only these, but so lovingly uttered,
   That they echoed for many a year
In the heart of the poor troubled mother,
   Who had poured out her sad tale of woe
To the teacher, "cum askin' fer Jimmie,"
   Who is down with a fever, you know.

Though "the leddy" was only a teacher,
   She was one of God's angels just then,
Of the brightest of ministering spirits
   Jimmie's teacher shone out among men!
And her ministry only was kindness,
   A few words, and a bright little smile,
But they lightened a poor mother's sadness
   In sharing her grief for awhile.

Only this, 'twas a word told " in season,"
    And as such was accepted in love,
As the lowliest deed done for Christ's sake
    Is accounted full worthy above.
All the little things done to His brethren
    Are a service done unto Him too ;
'Tis the spirit that makes the acts worthy,
    In the love and the goodwill to do.

Ah, yes, there ! in the Love is the secret ;
    Just the love which is mighty to bind
In soft sympathy all hearts together,
    And which shows us the way to be kind.
Just the love which will prompt the sweet comfort,
    Which can offer each small kindly deed,
And this is the lack in each heart and home
    Which creates such a general need.

It is love which can hurry us onward
    In the struggle to set the wrong right ;
The absence of love is the loss of strength,
    And without it we hinder the fight.
It is love which can soften the roughness,
    And take out the hardness of life,
Only this will bring pleasure and gladness
    To diminish earth's harrowing strife.

Only love can achieve man's salvation,
    Whose own will is as feeble as breath,
And the highest of loves is Eternal,
    The great Love which has overcome Death ;

And this Love, which we know is transcendant,
   Is Heaven's freest, most bountiful dower;
Should not we then, strive after possession
   Of this magical life-giving power?
Ah yes! and with this for our watchword,
   We will bravely do all that we may
To shed the love-light of a glorious Dawn
   O'er the darkness which heralds the day.

Marigolds--A Morning Song.

MARIGOLDS, marigolds, sunnily bright,
   Deep yellow, pale yellow, orange and white,
Wake from your slumbers to welcome the light,
   Fast fleeteth the night.

Marigolds, marigolds, blooming so fair,
Flowers of the Virgin, ah, what do ye there
Hiding the charms that should lighten all care?
   A charm I would share.

Marigolds, marigolds, daybreak is nigh,
Crimson and purple are changing the sky;
Silently, grandly, in cloud-cars on high,
   Aurora troops by.

Marigolds, marigolds, tell me, I pray,
Will a sweet maiden come hither to-day,
Plucking the blossoms so brilliant. so gay,
      That lie on her way?

Marigolds, marigolds, happy are ye,
All the loved grace of her beauty to see,
Sharing the bliss of her dear company,
      Light-hearted and free.

Marigolds, marigolds, tell her, my queen,
Lone and sad hearted I leave this fair green;
Duty must come before pleasure, I ween,
      Though Love come between.

Marigolds, marigolds, flowers of the sun,
Give me a blessing for work to be done;
Labour alone I no longer may shun;
      The day has begun.

Among the Shadows.

" ANY Flowers sir? Lovely spring blossoms !
        Is the cry of a poor weary lass,
And a bunch of damp faded violets
    Is held out to each one as they pass.
"They're only a penny the bunch, ma'am,
    And so cheap for the time of the year,"
A gloved hand just touches the pocket,
    But is lifted again, with " O dear !
I've no change just now, little flower girl,"
    And the child, disappointed, shrinks back,
She seemed so near getting a penny,
    And her business to-day was so slack.

A neighbouring clock is heard chiming,
    Slowly, clearly, the strokes ring out eight ;
Despairing, she looks at her basket,
    Scarcely eased of its full morning's weight.
With tears in her eyes she toils homewards,
    Yet can this be the home that she seeks ?
A tenement house in an alley,
    Where the air is so foul that it reeks
With noisome and pestilence vapours ;
    With a quick step the girl hastens in,
Unheeding the filth and the darkness,
    Caring naught for the clamorous din.

Her thoughts are all with her sick mother,
    So troubled, so hungry and ill ;
With a cry of welcoming gladness
    She enters, then frightened, stands still ;
The desolate garret is empty,
    And the girl turns away with a cry,
But a harsh voice breaks in with anger :
    "Come ! no creepin' in 'ere on the sly,
Yer mother 'as gone to the work 'us,
    Fer folks can't stop 'ere as don't pay,
I see yer've sold none o' them posies,
    So mind yer keep out o' *my* way !"

Out, out in the streets goes the beggar,
    Away in the cold and the rain,
Till the night-winds chill the poor body,
    And her heart is relieved of all pain.
A death in the workhouse, next morning,
    "Of starvation," on record we find,
And a child is found dead on the doorstep
    Of the woman who *meant* to be kind.
The child died "from cold and exposure"
    Is the rumour the papers report,
But death from the lack of friendly aid
    Is the verdict of Charity's Court.

Why should we Live?

Why should we live,
When death is such a sweet and blissful rest?
What has this life to offer that is best,
    Or even slightly better than fair death?
Tired are we, too weary yet to roam,
We woo thee, Death, to take us to our Home.

We love not life,
Its cares are toilsome, and its pathways steep,
Its burdens heavy. No, we long for sleep,
    A grave wherein to rest our wearied frames,
A welcome pillow in the humble sod,
Our one great yearning this : full rest with God.

Why should we live?
Because the Father wills it. Even so
'Tis ours to meekly bear the cross below,
    And in our bearing seek to prove our love
To Him Who made us all we have and are.
Should it our portion be, His work to mar?

Ah, this is Life,
To do the lovely Will of God, and win
The purest bliss hereafter to begin,
    The joys commencing which shall never cease ;
This is the fuller Life, the which to know
The highest blessing is, Heaven may bestow.

" There hath not failed."

THERE hath not failed
　　One word of all His promises so free !
Look up, my soul, this message is for thee.
　　　What have availed
Thy weakly murmurings at His wondrous way?
Faithfully hath He led thee day by day.
What though His path seemed sometimes rough and
　　　strange,
Hast thou not safely passed through many a change,
Grievous at first, afterwards doubly blest?
God knows, O troubled soul, what still is best,
In Christ, my weary spirit, find thy rest.

　　　With His Own Hand
He led thee from the darkness of thy sin ;
He still will guide thee till thou enterest in
　　　The Promised Land.
Now thou dost wander in the desert, till
Thou yieldest thee more fully to His Will ;
He wants thee, weary soul, to rest in Him,
Else thou must ever dwell where shades bedim
The vision, shades of deepest, saddest night
Of sin and worldliness, Heaven's pure clear light
Shines only o'er the path of truth and right.

Then yield, my soul,
To God, thine own true Lord and gracious King;
Yield all thyself, to Him more closely cling.
 He made thee whole,
He cleansed thee from thy leprosy of guilt,
He healed thee with His Life-blood, freely spilt
For all who like thyself were sick with woe;
He gave thee peace and hope. Dost thou not know
How surely *all* His promises are thine?
Oh, cease, my soul, to sinfully repine
Against a Will so graciously Divine.

 If thou hast known
His care and guidance throughout all Life's way,
Canst thou not further trust? and learn to say:
 " My sin I own;
Forgive me, Father, if I yet may dare
Still to approach Thy throne in simple prayer.
Thou hast been faithful to Thy promised word,
I have been faithless. Lord, my heart is stirred
Within me in contrition deep, sincere;
I crave for pardon. Wilt Thou deign to hear
My low petition? Yes, I need not fear!

 " I seek Thine aid,
Thy sympathy and comfort, sweet indeed,
Never with-holden from Thy child in need. ·
 I am afraid,
Fearful without Thee, sorely needing strength
And courage for the Future's dreary length,
The path of Life, so different to tread
Alone, with unknown dangers far ahead;

Oh Lord, Who thus hast promised, be my Guide,
Be with me always, let me e'er abide
In Thee, and in Thy safe Pavilion hide.

    "Thy promise, Lord,
Is precious to my weary fainting heart,
In all my grief, I know Thou hadst a part;
    The holy cord
Of threefold sympathy is thus more sure.
What fears I have, Thou shared them all before,
For all my trouble, all my load of care,
Thou in humanity didst take Thy share,
And in Thy love and mercy still wilt take
An interest in the daily prayers I make,
My Father, hear me now, for Jesu's sake;

    "Amen, and Peace!"
Thus pray, my troubled spirit, hour by hour
While still surrounded by temptation's power,
    Till death release
Thee gladly from thy sin-dimmed dwelling place;
Pray, and in faith, for God's great gift of grace,
Grace to sustain thee through the ills of life,
Grace to uplift thee from its weary strife,
Above its sinful, all-bespoiling mire;
Sufficient Grace to bear thee ever higher,
Nearer to Christ, thy one supreme desire!

After many Days.

AFTER the long, long drought
  Falls the refreshing rain,
Scattering gems from the darkened skies
  To gladden the earth again.

Veiled is the summer sun,
  Veiled in a rain-wrought mist,
Hiding its glow where the clouds lie thick
  Alone by its warm rays kissed.

Softly the leaf-hung trees
  Bend with a thankful grace,
Gladly receiving the welcome showers
  With a quiv'ring, long embrace.

Joyous, the flowers uplift
  Their gaily fashioned bells
To gather the pearl-drops pure and fair
  Now glist'ning across the dells.

Th' fields with their harvest hopes
  Wave in the gentle wind,
Breathing, in faith for the promised math,
  The drops for their growth assigned.

So " after many days "
  Of trusting hope long tried,
The rainbow shines for our Faith's reward
  And Nature's joy and pride.

So " after many days,"
  Fulfilment fair and sweet
Falls to the lot of earth's every son,
  Faith's promise to complete.

So " after many days,"
  Though sadly long and drear,
The promised joy shall be given to all,
  Our longing hearts to cheer.

The Home of Childhood.

THE unbroken links of our family chain
  Gird heart to heart with affection still,
No sorrow, nor trial, nor grief, nor pain
  The warmth of our love can chill.

Grim Death, the divider of human loves
  Has passed from us with an empty hand,
And only the mark of his noisome gloves
  Is left as Memory's brand.

We thank Thee, our God, for our well-filled haunt
   Of youthful spirits and parent hearts ;
We joy in the love which can bravely daunt
   Deep Misery's keenest darts.

We welcome Thy blessing of inward peace,
   And crave but an undiminished share
Of Thy purest Love in its great increase,
   To render our lives more fair.

Ah ! What in all Life will excel the charm
   We young folks find in our father's home ?
And foolish are we when we venture harm
   In longing the world to roam.

Though our after life may be fair and sweet,
   Beneath will roll the deep undertone
Of regret for the joys of the old retreat,
   The home we have loved and known.

But we cherish still in its dear disguise
   This earthly type of our final Rest,
And offer thanks for the Heaven-sent prize
   Of our home so fully blest.

Mysterious Love.

T HERE is happiness in being lovéd,
　　A charm as pure as the early dew,
As sweet as rose-scent flowing windward,
As fair as all the joys of Summer,
Fair and sweet and grandly true;
Happiness beyond all measure,
Deeper than the oceaned treasure,
Deeper than the unfathomed seas
With their unknown wealth abounding,
Where above the waves roll onward
Heedless of the wealth below them
As the steady undercurrents
Flow unheeding every wavelet,
In the vigour of their ease
Spurning every passing breeze.

There is happiness in all Love's bounty,
And where we love we hold the greatest peace.
To give is always better than receiving,
And giving love is but a good investment
Whose quick returns must evermore increase;
And when we love we lay up endless riches,
Not to be counted in this sin soiled world,
But reckoned only in that great Forever
Which lies before us, in deep mystery furled,
Whose strange existence we but dimly guess at,
Led to surmises by the wants of nature,
Our love-bathed nature, which compels the soul
To look to, hope for, an eternal life-love's goal.

There is sadness too in loving truly,
A sadness sweet, though sweet in pain,
Having no darkness in its sorrow,
For only doubt has aught of darkness,
And Love is bright as the sunbeam's skein,
The golden web that adorns the earth,
And casts its charm on the meadows green,
And over the ocean's changing scene,
With impartial glory and glowing worth,
The golden skein of the countless years
That sum up the past, and bring to men
The wealth of the sunshine that wasted then,
And scattered its treasures as we shed tears;
But the tears and the beams of that ancient Sun
Have neither been lost.   Ah ! no, not one
Of those pitiful tears we shed in grief,
As we yearned o'er the friend, and gave relief
By our deep compassion to him we loved,
Not one of those scattered tears was lost;
The pity was sweet and the Love excelled
The costliest treasure man ever held.
The Love was Heaven's own special dower
Sent to illumine Life's darkest hour,
And a light is always a worthy sign
No matter how feebly its rays may shine;
It may beam from the casket of gold embossed,
Or flare from the lantern of dullest tin,
So Love gleams out in the haunts of sin
As well as the halls of the proudly good
So high in their conscious rectitude.

Yes, there is anxious pain in loving truly,
For the light gleams over a world of care,
And Love finds ever some grief to share,
A grief more deep as it falls on those
We fain would screen from all sorrow-blows;
And Life can never be all of Love,
For where we love, the world may hate
And the dear one wrestles with adverse fate
Which chills like an ice-bite the noon of youth,
Or the shady evening of growing age ;
And the heart has sometimes the bitter wage
Of cold suspicion for Love's own truth.

But there *is* Happiness in being lovéd,
And Happiness in purely loving too,
And Love fulfills its only perfect mission
In sharing those deep griefs, and greater sorrows
Of all we love, in all we find most true.
Pain must be blent with all of earth's perfections,
Else what were Heaven itself to bear in view ?
And if we love, this pain is still the sweetest,
As pain must ever be when shared with love;
Till in our Soul's complete and last fruition,
We learn the meaning of the mystic bond
Of grief and love, which now but closes darkly
Before our mental vision,—and beyond,
Beyond the doubts and cares that vex us now,
We all shall *know*, and in our knowledge bow
Before Him, in the deepest, fullest Love,
Before Him, our great Father, God above.

The Power of a Song.

THE factory bell has rung, the massive gates swing
   wide,
  Release the surging sea of human souls;
A seldom ceasing, restless, ebbing, flowing tide;
   Troubled, tempestuous, rarely calm, it rolls
Forward or backward, as the chiming hours decide.

Wearily, sullenly, the crowd sways slowly on,
   And, rising over all, a murmurous din
Echoes, re-echoes, till the mighty throng has gone,
   Each to his search for pleasure, rest or sin,
Seeking and finding till a new day dawns anon.

Still thus receding, and to-day a hush comes first;
   Scarce but a moment is the way deterred,
As tones of sweetest music over all have burst,
   Holding the listeners, as they catch each word,
Silently spell-bound, ev'n the most depraved, the worst.

Only a low, sweet song. The crowd makes way again,
   Leaving the singer with her work of love;
And yet she casts her angel-message not in vain,
   Her presence breathes a pureness from Above,
Her song holds safety in its fair, harmonious strain.

Only a woman's voice singing the well-known hymn :
  "Abide with me, fast falls the eventide ;"
Only a weary toiler in the twilight dim
  Saved from intended sin, who else had died,
Strangely redeemed from shame and sorrow, darkly
    grim.

Only old memories, thus brought back to some few
    hearts,
  Of long past days, and words, unheeded then,
Come with a welcome power as present gloom departs,
  Soothing with gentle Peace the griefs of men,
Tenderly, slowly, with Love's graceful, healing arts.

Our Rocky Cornish Coast.

LOUDLY sounds the breakers' roar
    Dashing 'gainst the rocky shore,
Whirling eddies to the fore,
    Backed by rolling surge ;

Rising, falling, wreathed in white,
Swelling, foaming, as with spite,
On they rush with awful might
    To the cliffs' steep verge ;

Overwhelming, with their spray,
Precipice so rough and grey,
Then receding, mocking, gay,
    Toward the open sea.

Staunch and firm, our rocks so bold
Stand as warriors stood of old,
When the war cry round them rolled
    On the battle-field.

Stable, stern, unto the last,
Will our rocks stand, true and fast,
Ever braving storm and blast,
    Cornwall's hardy shield.

Surging waves with ceaseless song,
Steadfast ramparts still and strong,
Always to our shores belong,
    Fortress of the free !

The Charm of Beauty.

H OW strangely sweet it is to note our world
    Apparently more lovely day by day,
And yet we know the change is not around,
But in ourselves. Nature has ever held
In her fair bosom many a mystery,
A hidden power of wondrous loveliness.

Yes, as the years pass on, and seasons change,
In each new opening flower afresh we note
Evidence of a lovely harmony.
The mystic growth of every budding tree,
The soft green grass glist'ning with morning dew,
Late Autumn's varied tints and ruddy glows,
How purely fair with all entrancing charm
These in good sooth appear! And yet again,
The dawn of day, the twilight's shadowy hour,
The peaceful beauty of the river-path,
Old restless ocean with his myriad waves
Fringed with the gleaming sand of many a shore,
These several scenes, widely diversified,
Each in its point of pleasure singular,
Strike with new interest our awakened sight.
But oh, how oft our better nature sleeps,
And hideous phantoms people all our sphere,
Imaginations of a mind diseased,
Disordered by our wilful apathy.
Ah, never should we passively permit
The dark'ning shadows of our troubled lives,
The dull black clouds of trial to hide from us
These beautiful alleviations, given
That man may not grow soulless, cramped or mean ;
But filled with that free life, fair nature's gift,
He must perforce expand, a healthy soul,
Till, on the wings of immortality,
He soars above the world, its strife, its care,
A Conqueror, to fairer realms beyond !

To Mother--A Birthday Greeting.

SHOULD a loving birthday greeting
    Find its seal in glistening tears?
Yet the deepest heart emotions
    Meet no other silent peers.
Oh, that I might heal your sorrow,
    And allay your present fears;
This indeed were fairest offering
    For the coming changeful years.

But my earnest supplications
    Always soar in loving faith
Up to God Whose holy mercies
    Shall your every hour enswathe,
Up to Him Whose power immortal
    Holds the issues of our breath,
Up to Him Whose Love eternal
    Gladdens Life and conquers Death.

I can offer little, Mother
    As a birthday gift to-day,
Little are all earthly favours
    To the full supporting sway
Of our Father's richest tendresse,
    Christian's only certain stay;
With that Love to light you, dearest,
    You will need no meaner ray.

H

But I know you cherish fondness,
　　Even smallest earthly lights,
Lights of dim and flickering vapour
　　Scarcely stars in Life's dark nights;
Then accept the earnest wishes
　　Which a loving heart indites,
And forgive their trembling fervour
　　In your love's compassionate flights.

Night on the Harbour.

NIGHT on the harbour, calm, fairest night,
　　Hushing to slumber the cares of the light,
Shading serenely the woes of the day,
Veiling its glare in a soft mist of grey;
Night on the Harbour, so peaceful in sorrow,
Taking its rest for the cares of the morrow.

Night on the harbour, soberly drest,
Comes it in silence, an all-welcome guest,
Welcome and beautiful, shadowed but fair,
Lit by the glory its shadows prepare;
High in her cloud-land the Queen-moon reclining,
Gladdens the earth with the grace of her shining.

Night on the harbour, lit with the sheen
Of countless bright twinklings the vessels between ;
Over the waters their radiance is shed,
Reflecting with beauty the brilliance o'erhead ;
Yonder in cloudland the moon-rays are gleaming,
Here o'er the waters the ships' lights are streaming.

Night on the harbour, calm, fairest night,
In shadow-robes glowing, in dark stillness bright,
Rest o'er the waters, and peace in the sky,
Peace where the moon's grey-clad servitor's lie,
Rest on the harbour where night lingers slowly,
Sweet peaceful night in all restfulness holy !

Summer's Passing.

SEPTEMBER.

HEARD you the winds wildly crying?
  Note ye the breezes soft sighing?
They tell us that Summer is dying,
  The Summer is passing away !

List that the birds cease their singing,
The hill-sides no echoes are ringing,
Our songsters their flight are now winging,
  To the South are they hasting to-day.

The flowers in the woodland are faded ;
The long forest-path grows less shaded ;
The leaves to the earth are degraded,
    So withered to rot and decay.

The brooks tell a weird, wintry story ;
The meadows have lost their gay glory ;
They change, and ere long will be hoary,
    All mantled in icy array.

O, hark to the ocean's dull sobbing,
With a sound as if it were robbing
The note of my weary heart's throbbing,
    Th' horizon is heavy and gray.

My soul is o'erladen with sorrow,
And nature my grief seems to borrow,
For Winter is coming to-morrow
    To banish the Summer away.

DECEMBER.

The long sunny days have departed,
But Winter has proved kindly-hearted,
Has soothèd the wounds which once smarted
    In dread of his own frosty reign.

Methinks I still hear a bird singing ;
Yes, there on that leafless bough swinging,
Though not leafless, the ivy is clinging
    To the sturdy oaks in the lane.

The leaves with the rain-drops are gleaming,
Down the road, tiny rivers are streaming,
And I peacefully rest, idly dreaming
    O'er the past with its fear and pain.

Robin sings a message so cheery
To all who are troubled and weary;
He sings that the days now are dreary,
    But Summer is coming again!

Our Creator's Love.

H AS earth no pleasures that we spend our days
    Mourning and sighing over past delight?
Surely the fears which turn our noon to night
Would all disperse, could we but learn to raise
Maybe the feeblest song of heartfelt praise
    To God, our loving Father, Lord of might,
    Maker and King;—praise for the wondrous height
And depth of Love which He to us displays.
Is there no pleasure? Have we naught but pain?
    Is there no joy we know is ours indeed?
Is there—? But why prolong the doleful strain?
    There is a joy our every joy above,
Far more exceeding ev'n our greatest need,
    The present, future joy of God's vast Love!

Of every love the free abundant source,
    God's Love,—all knowing, self-contained, supreme,
    The centre of Creätion's grandest theme,
Of every power the ever-potent force—
Stands high above the strongest magnet's course,
    Higher than worlds on worlds, stream over stream
    Of starry firmaments in glory's gleam,
Whose highest splendours but this Love endorse.
    God's Life, eternal essence, Love alone
It stands, and ever stood, and evermore
Remains the boundless ocean whose wide shore
No foot may reach, no wing may ever soar,
    Nor knowledge grasp its all-encircling zone,
    The sea of Love our Father calls His Own.

Fatherhood.

THE first-born son was his father's pride,
  But the baby's life was the mother's death.
 At his first weak cry she resigned her breath;
His life her last offering ere she died,
  And he was his father's well-loved son,
  The only one.

He lisped his prayers at his father's knee,
  Told his baby griefs to a manly ear;
  And Time passed on, adding year to year,
Till the babe attained to a youth's degree,
  And the years were passed at his father's side,
  No love denied.

But the only son reached manhood's prime,
  And longed in his vigour after life;
  He yearned for the bustle and eager strife
Of the busy world of a stirring time;
  And the father mourned, yet concealed his grief
  For th' son's relief.

He bade him go, and an anguished sigh,
　　And many a wrestling with bitter pain,
　　Were the only signs of the heart's great strain.
His great love conquered, he said goodbye,
　　And bravely hid his deep grief away
　　In love's array.

So the son went forth to the life he craved,
　　With the untried strength of a quiet youth.
　　He found much life in a guise uncouth,
But not th' ideal his dreams engraved ;
　　His Fancy's visions were soon distraught,
　　And fall'n to naught.

And he battled there with many a sin,
　　And drank full deep of the world's mixed draught.
　　He lived with men of a wealthy craft,
And was quickly snared in the gilded gin
　　Which th' Tempter sets for unwary feet,
　　Too free, too fleet.

But he bought his wisdom with his fall,
　　Till he learnt the task Experience gives
　　To her careless pupils.　(He who lives
To avoid her most learns more than all,
　　For she is the sternest judge to those
　　Who shun her blows).

He rose again, and the years passed on.
　　He learnt to love, and he ceased to roam ;
　　He wedded well, and possessed a home ;
A wiser man for the follies gone,
　　But not unscathed by the ruthless past,
　　The scars will last.

The love he knew was a clear bright flame,
 Whose zeal inspired the highest good,
 And the fullest grace of manlihood
Grew o'er the past with its sin and blame.
 His life shone fair for the future years,
 Undimmed by fears.

While in lonely grief the father yearned
 With unlessened love for his only child.
 Beholders saw that he rarely smiled,
But no one knew how his great heart burned
 With the long desires of an unmet love,
 Known but Above.

His thin, bent frame grew frailer yet;
 The sad wan face was pale with age;
 He turned the last and the shortest page
Of his volumed life, and ceased to fret.
 He lay with patience awaiting rest,
 In calmness drest.

He awaited death; while the son clasped joy
 In its gladdest presence, and life was fair.
 He lived, he loved, and the treasure rare
Of a true home life, without one alloy,
 Was his in truth; and he had a son,
 His well-loved one.

And the babe's caress on his manly face,
 Its clinging weakness and helpless mien,
 Constrained in him all Love's wish to screen
His boy from the sins of an erring race;
 And within the love of new fatherhood,
 He understood;

Aye, he understood his own parent's heart,
    And the pain and sadness so bravely borne
    From the early hours of his own birth morn,
From the first receipt of that greatest dart,
    The mother's death, to the last neglect;
    A life-joy wreckt.

And he, the son, had increased the ill,
    That terrible wound of his father's grief;
    Who should have been first to lend relief
Had but confirmed the lonely chill
    Which th' saddened heart had sustained so long,
    In love so strong.

Ah! he knew all now.   At his baby's cot
    The bitterest wisdom of life was gained;
    The knowledge learnt of a great heart pained
And wrung in bearing the weary lot
    Of husband and father twice bereaved,
    And doubly grieved.

And this knowledge gained; was it won too late?
    To be but a burden of useless woe?
    Was it only learnt that it might but show
How weak is the creature who plays with Fate,—
    The Fate that is ruled by an all-just God,
    His avenging Rod—?

The worldly son, in his hours of joy,
    Had known that his father aged and failed,
    Though he scarce had guessed how the body ailed
Through the heart's deep care for the errant boy,
    And now in repentance he feared the worst:
    Would death be first?

The worn old man had reached the end,
　　And his lonely heart was full of peace.
　　The call of death would but mean release,
A gift from the hand of a new-found friend ;
　　And a worthy gift, although meanly wrapped,
　　And roughly strapped.

But within his heart, and amid the calm
　　Of his waiting-time, he ceased not to pray
　　For the absent son, till the shadows grey
Of the final hour came, with the psalm
　　And the evening hymn of an old church nigh,
　　Echoing by.

The gentle clouds of the Summer's night
　　Curtained the glow of the glorious West,
　　And the father whispered : " It is best.
The next fair dawn shall be Heaven's light."
　　And he ceased his prayers for the well-loved son ;
　　" God's Will be done."

God's Will is gracious, and full of love.
　　Weak man in sin may oppose that Will,
　　And try to disguise it with his ill,
But God is watching, unmoved, above,
　　And His is ever the Will supreme,
　　Man's but a dream.

The shadows fell into deepest gloom,
　　And the old man's breath grew weakly hushed,
　　As he lay with his life-joy almost crushed,
Welcoming death as the brightest doom ;
　　Till a step was heard on the nearest stair—
　　His son was there !

The light returned to those long-dimmed eyes,
    A happy smile to the wrinkled face,
    And the shades of death for a brief, bright space
Were drawn aside, in the glad surprise,
    As the great re-union dulled past pain
    To th' father's gain.

There were words of grief for the son to speak,
    While honest tears made tiny streams
    Adown the course of the troubled seams
That marked the care on his world-worn cheek ;
    But the words were brave, and the tears were true,
    And manly too.

The father checked with his wavering voice
    The self-reproaches the son poured out,
    And chid the strain of a worthless doubt
That he half-surmised, and said : " What choice
    " Would you make, my son, if you wished to live :
    " Hate or forgive ?

" If your little lad in an hour of blame
    " Reproached himself for the sins he owned,
    " And never a single fault condoned,
" Would you bear him scorn in his grief and shame ?
    " Would you hate him still for the follies gone,
    " Hate, and live on ?

" Or would you not love him but the more,
    " Your one wee child, for the faults confest ?
    " Love him, and shed to the air the rest,
" The shame, and the sin, and the whole sad store ? "
    " Love him ? Ah, is he not my child ? "
    And each one smiled.

"And if, my son, you would thus forgive
  "In the freest love of your parent-heart,
  "Why should not I, who have but to part?
"If you would love while you yet may live,
  "Why not myself, who have but to die?
  "Ah, may not I?"

The son bowed down his strong self, and wept,
  His warm tears bathing the old man's hand.
  "At last, my father, I understand;"
He whispered low, and the father slept
  With a smile on his face, as his spirit passed
  To rest at last.

Chrysanthemums.

                Chrysanthemum!
The season's latest trophy; thee we hail
With rapturous ecstasy. Thy many tints
Are varied as the rainbow's beauteous hues,
Or, as the glowing sky at break of day,
In morning splendour wrapt. Can aught excel
Thy pure and snowy blossoms wondrous fair,
And those bright golden gems, so freely poured

Upon us by the Autumn's brilliant sun,
Assisted by a frequent copious shower
Of soft refreshing rain? Thy purple blooms
Could vie with any ancient, regal robes
Of solemn grandeur, and of sumptuous state,
Or with the vaporous mantle, which enfolds
The hills when morning dawns. Thy crimson flowers
Can only be compared with sunset's glow,
And the deep lustre of the ruby fair
Caught by a passing ray of glittering light,
Or golden sunbeam. All our flowers are sweet,
But none more dear than thee, Chrysanthemum,
Blooming when they are faded, when the wind
Plays ruthlessly among thy coloured balls,
Tossing them here and there with fierce, rough glee,
Yet adding to their strength. But words are vain
To speak of all thy brilliant lights and shades.
The glowing picture of the garden, gay
With thy bright blossoms, numberless and rare,
Is ever better seen than thus described.
Farewell, we whisper. While the wild wind blows,
Bloom on in hardy beauty, lovely strength,
Our latest Autumn star, Chrysanthemum.

The Approach of Winter.

THE trees are thinning, thinning,
　　The nights grow long and chill,
The breeze is rough, and the leaves fall fast,
　　And never the brook is still,
The rains have swoll'n the torrent,
　　And shattered the forest's dress,
The trees show bare 'gainst the shifting clouds
　　So cold in their cheerlessness.

Winter is coming, coming,
　　Laden with snow and storm,
But Inglenook is our safe retreat,
　　So lovingly, gaily warm.
The frosts shall gem the windows,
　　And the snows may drape the earth,
But Home is bright, and our own hearth side
　　Shall echo with happy mirth.

The wind is blowing, blowing,
　　Telling of want and care,
And sad'ning tales of a woeful need
　　Are whispered throughout the air ;
But Love shall be our safeguard,
　　The Love that is shed from Heaven,
And 'mid the warmth of our brightest hours
　　We must heed the hunger-driven.

Winter is coming, coming,
   Its days may bring us woe ;
Who knows the griefs that sweep with its storms,
   Or come with the drifting snow?
But braced with true heart vigour
   As stern as the frosty rime,
We will bravely meet the fiercest blast
   That sharpens the wings of Time.

The Last Word.

" A WEARY, so weary," the tired lips sigh,
   And the eyelids in heaviness close;
There's never a pillow to rest the worn head,
   To invite the much needed repose.
The monotonous whirr of the big machines,
   And the workers' dull undertones,
Are the only music to lull her to sleep,
   To accompany her desolate moans.

In the darkest recess of the well-filled room
   Disregarded she strives with her pain,
The anguish of knowing her work is undone,
   A long toil of such requisite gain ;

And despite the relief of enforcéd rest,
    Her soul wears itself in deep sighs;
The mother knows well, in her heart's loving care,
    Who must suffer and want if she dies.

It is well for herself, the quick coming sleep,
    The repose of a peaceful death,
And but for her children, the spirit's one joy
    Would be but to yield up her breath,
To rest her worn self in the cold, silent arms
    Of the last and unchangeable sleep,
To loosen her hold upon earth's weary cares,
    And under death's shelter to creep.

But her babes! Ah, here the true motherly heart
    Shrinks back to the struggle of life;
She would rather work on in her weakness and pain
    In the maze of continuous strife,
If but, by so doing, her babes might be fed,
    If only their cries might be hushed;
But the frame is too weak for the toil she craves,
    The spirit too certainly crushed.

The noise of the workers grows fainter; the rays
    Of the gas-light are lost in deep gloom;
The cares and the pains in the distance grow less
    As she slowly approaches the tomb.
The *tomb?* Ah, yet nothing so sombre and sad
    Encloses the prospect she meets,
But only a peace and a new, holy joy
    Is impent in the future she greets.

No thought of a death-tomb could call forth the peace
   That fills her poor heart with such rest ;
Almost with a smile she has laid down her head,
   And welcomed the grave, silent guest.
Her chill face is laid on the half-sewn work,
   Where the needle glints out from the band ;
A thimble shines brightly against the wan blue
   Of her rigid and death-cold hand ;

But the look of deep peace still covers the face,
   And no din may disturb that peace now ;
The last whispered word of those fixed, pallid lips
   Is the "*Rest*" that has lightened her brow.
The monotonous whirr of the big machines
   Rolls on in unceasing din,
But the one worn worker has rest at last,
   In her final " Entering in."

The Dead and the Living.

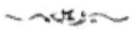

WE weep for the silent dead,
    Who rest in the long calm sleep
Of the peaceful grave, until Time's last wave ;
    For the silent dead we weep.

But oh! For the living still,
　By th' burdens of life o'er pressed,
We shed not a tear; yet the sorrows here
　Are worse than the long sweet rest.

The dust in the grave we mourn,
　And sigh for the soul now fled;
We cast not a thought on the blessing wrought
　In th' peace of the silent dead;

And the living hearts may ache,
　Lie crushed with the awful pain
Of a sad life-day, while we turn away
　To ponder the tombs again.

We weep for the silent dead,
　But let us just breathe a prayer
For the living too, with their work to do,
　And sorrow and grief to bear.

Yes, weep for the silent dead,
　And help the poor mourners here,
That the sad, worn heart, till its griefs depart,
　May yet have a joy to cheer.

Yes, pray while the quick tears fall,
　Work while we moan and sigh,
And with lives we bless in their bitterness
　Our saddest griefs shall die.

Evening Thoughts.

GENTLY and softly, as the day is dying,
    The evening breezes faintly waft to me,
'Mid the harmonious forest-trees' low sighing,
    The fragrant perfume of the flowery lea,
And the sweet music of the birds now hieing
    To rest, beneath the shady old oak tree.

Over the well-worn bridge I slowly wander,
    Pausing awhile above the shallow brook
Through treasured memories to my heart grown fonder
    Than many a prettier, less secluded nook,
While up amid the leafy foliage yonder
    I note the eyrie of a watchful rook.

And staying thus, I gently fall aweeping,
    Yet not for present cares or troubling woe,
Rather at all the old dreams round me sweeping,
    Sad souvenirs of those one used to know,
Friends now beneath the turf so calmly sleeping,
    Or parted by the ocean's ebb and flow.

Ah me ! The world is dreary, as thus musing
   I let past joys bedim my clouded sight,
And all the blessings of my lot abusing,
   Regretful *might-have-beens* obscure Heaven's light ;
For a brief space, all peace and calm refusing,
   I sadly mourn o'er things which once were bright.

But oh ! I wake me from this sinful dreaming
   To better thoughts of joys that are to be.
My God, forgive my sin in ever deeming
   My burden here aught but what's best for me,
For well I know its darkness is but seeming,
   Thy smile is there, a sure reality.

Over my spirit blessed peace is stealing,
   The peace to murmuring hearts alone denied,
And from the church I hear the sweet bells pealing,
   Chiming the twilight hour ; my steps they guide
Till in God's House I whisper, humbly kneeling,
   " I know there shall be light at Eventide."

A Problem.

THE inner I, what is it? Who can tell?
    Not ev'n my spirit's self.   I only know
It was of God, once like Himself, once pure,
But now defiled by many a year of sin,
And dressed in fashion's every paltry sham;
Only it once was born of God, and still
Before Him, in His just and holy sight,
Can bear the impress, feebly though it rests,
Of what the Soul once knew, and what it was.

How can I understand myself, who know
So little else of all that makes up life?
I, who may see a simple blade of grass,
May pluck it, tear it into emerald gems,
Yet cannot tell the mystery of its growth,
Yet may not give to it the bloom I marred,
Never restore it to its own sweet grace.

How can I know myself, who know of Life
So much, and yet so little, all in all?
So much, that I am weary with its strife,
Wearied to sadness with its fret and woe,
Wearied of battling with the knowledge gained
In darker shades of sin, weary of toil,
In seeking to condense the huge, weird mass

Of independent fact, and larger dreams,
And trying to arrange their many lines
To something of a serviceable use;
So much, too much of life's illusive gain,
That in the knowledge I have lost myself,
And only here and there can claim to meet
The God-like image that I yearn to call
My one and only self, the one true *me*.
And yet so little do I know of life,
So little, and so much there is to know;
I cannot understand the smallest turn
Of Time's sure cycle. Wherefore? how? and what?
Are queries still that vainly I may strive
To answer, but I find no key thereto.

There is an outer *I*, that acts and talks,
Aye, even sometimes thinks. The world has known
This self, and so presumes it thus knows all;
But still there is the personality,
The inner consciousness that came of God,
The only soul which I would call myself,
And this it is, which, though I scarce may know
The wondrous motor of its one great power,
Can influence in its all of good or ill
The outer life that screens its inward flow.
This, the true soul, concealed in many a guise,
Marred and deformed by many a tyrant sin,
Yet has its power, its love and God-given life.
It came from God, and will one nearing day
Return to Him Who gave it all its love,
Its power, its hope and faith, its endless Life.

Clouds.

THE white mist is shrouding the sleeping earth,
  Concealing its burdens of joy and care ;
Nature a new day is bringing to birth
  Beneath the soft coverlet resting there.
The night cloud falls, a mysterious veil
  Between the world and the far-away sky,
Vainly we pierce its invincible pale,
  It baffles the glance of the human eye.

But Faith can perceive the herald of day,
  Though hidden by clouds from our longing sight,
She knows when the mists shall have passed away,
  The earth will rejoice in the glad sunlight.
Darkness may linger around the grey hills,
  The soft mist gather in valley and glen,
Yet a bird his song for the morning trills,
  Rebuking the faithless distrust of men.

Silently, slowly, the mist will soon fade,
  The night-clouds melt and the gloom disappear,
The day stand forward in glory arrayed,
  With garments of sunbeams brilliantly clear
The shadows will surely give way at last,
  No matter how long to the earth they cling,
Their sadness grow but a thought of the past
  In the pure, glad brightness the dawn will bring.

Read you my meaning? The mists of this life,
   Disguising Heaven's light to our partial view,
Are the sorrows deep, and the sins so rife,
   Are the night-clouds dark'ning the sparkling hue
Of the wide expanse of God's glorious Love;
   So we oftimes fail through the deepening gloom
To perceive the light still shining above,
   And sadly repine at our fancied doom.

But the Dawn will come, and the night will end;
   Already Faith's songsters can blithely chant
Their carols of joy, and their songs portend
   A sign of the bliss where Love's bright beams glant.
We need not fear at the darkness o'erhead,
   Preceding the dawn is the darkest hour;
We shall all rejoice when the clouds have sped,
   And gladly exult in the daylight's power.

As the World grows Old.

WHEN our youths have grown to manhood,
    And the babes are sturdy boys,
Then there comes the chilly feeling
    In the void of present joys,
And all life seems somewhat cold
As the world grows old.

When our girls make wives and mothers,
    And our smallest lass is grown,
When the nursery is forsaken,
    And the hearth is still and lone,
Then our life seems somewhat cold
As the world grows old.

When the times are changed and varied,
    And old friends are known no more,
When so many loved ones beckon
    From the farther, brighter shore,
Then this life seems very cold
And the world grows old.

When our limbs are bent and feeble
    And the pulse is faint and low,
When the weary eyes are dimmest
    And the tears for weakness flow,
Then our life seems just as cold
As the world is old.

But the spirit-world seems brighter
    For the dark'ning shades of earth,
And our love for all is higher
    By the chastening sorrow-birth,
And though life around grows old
Yet the heart is never cold.

The Coming of the Storm.

AT first the sunshine of a wintry day
    Brilliant and brief, the sky soon turns to grey,
Dark masses of dull cloud its surface spread,
A sickly hue o'er all the fields is shed ;
Mournfully whistling through the leafless trees
Colder and wilder blows the north-west breeze,
The birds in terror seek their sheltered nests ;
A strange dark shadow o'er the ocean rests,
The seething waves beat out their troubled dirge,
The melancholy sobbing of the surge,
Amid the heaving billows' undertone,
Sending through many a cave an echoing moan.

A moment's calm, sudden and strangely still,
With cold discomfort seems our world to fill ;
Above, the clouds roll on with silent frown,

Below, the sea reflects its dull dark brown,
And Nature everywhere suspends her breath,
Marking a pause as still as voiceless death.

It ceases ; louder blows the wind again,
One piercing gust sweeps round with fitful cry,
The clouds sweep wildly 'cross the leaden sky,
And swiftly falls the shower of sleet and rain.
Down from the Heaven's expanse long overcast,
And driven far before the strength-bound blast,
Driven in fury o'er the wind-lashed waves,
Scattering the seaweed in the low, dark caves,
Now pushing land-ward, with the boisterous wind,
Like a grim gaoler following sharp behind,
Smiting with chilly batteries the fields,
Shedding profusely all a storm-shower yields,
Carelessly through the remnants of the day
The wintry storm and tempest takes its way.

Below and Beyond.

BELOW the clouds is the sad, sad earth,
 With its burden of grief, and its tale of woe,
With its transient joys and its fleeting mirth ;
 Ah, these are the lot of the world below.

Beyond the clouds is the land of bliss,
 Where no trouble can enter, no sin defile,
And the sorrowing heart can look on to this :
 Its pleasures are ours in a little while.

Below the clouds is the darkest night,
 And the stars are few, and their radiance small ;
The vigil is long, and the hours' slow flight
 Is dreary and sad as the moments fall.

Beyond the clouds is the end of Time,
 No dials mark hours in Eternity's day ;
The sun never sets in the glorious clime
 Of the city whose King is its fairest Ray.

Below the clouds is the grind of toil,
 Deep harassing care and anxiety's load ;
No exemption is found from the Tempter's coil,
 As we slowly traverse earth's tiring road.

Beyond the clouds is our home of rest,
　Where we lay our burdens of weariness down,
And sin never enters the undefiled breast
　Of one who is wearing a victor's crown.

Below the clouds there are tears and sighs,
　And agonized partings from those we hold dear,
The relinquishment of the joys we most prize,
　The decay of hope and the growth of fear.

Beyond the clouds is the meeting-place
　Of loved ones long parted, where heart-breaking grief
Gives way to the blessings of sweet holy grace,
　And woeful despair to a gracious relief.

Below the clouds does our path lie still,
　Though never for long shall we share its strife ;
At the blessed recall of our Father's Will
　We shall gain the measure of highest Life.

Beyond the clouds we shall rise at last,
　To exist throughout the unchangeable years
In the active joys of Eternity vast,
　With the peace that calms, and the Love that cheers.

Below, beyond ! The comparison
　Is our greatest aid as we struggle beneath,
And the conflicts we suffer till life is done
　Are fittest to earn us the victor's wreath.

So faint not, worn heart, though the way be steep,
　The crown is awaiting the conqueror's brow ;
A little more battle, a brief dreamless sleep,
　And the joys beyond shall thy soul endow.

Life is Worth Living.

LIFE is worth living, yes, ah, truly yes!
  Though death be sweeter, life has still its sweets,
The pure and holy pleasure which entreats
The heart's repose, and leads us into joy.
Life is worth *living* in the truest sense,
Worth the great effort for the highest Life,
Worth the deep battle in a spirit's strife
To lead us conquerors in valiant right,
To lead us higher than Earth's sin-dark night
Into the morning of Heaven's righteousness.

Life is worth living for its glorious powers,
The spirit's yearning after better things,
The restless soul that soars on many wings
Into the realm of true Divinity,
And from that soaring, so deterred by sin,
It takes an impress of the Life Divine
That spurred it into rising, and that sign,
The outward mark of all the inner needs,
Stands far above man's wordy, petty creeds,
And purifies the soul it thus endowers.

Life is worth living, for our life below,
Marred by the stains of many a bitter sin,
Dimmed by the sorrows that have entered in,
Is but a training for the Life above,
That Life beyond, so far above the clouds
Of sin and doubt that soil existence here,
And if the training home seems oft times drear,
Is it aught but our own misguided wills
That cause the sorrows, make the bitter ills,
And cloud the whole of life with needless woe?

Life *is* worth living; life, of all the best,
Is worth the highest deeds we may sustain,
Is worth the quiet bearing of much pain
And sorrow, just because it is a life
And must for ever be the noblest gift.
So when our Maker chose to call mankind
Out of the soulless dust, to him He assigned
The fullest destiny in Nature given :
A life to hold on earth, and this once riven
The highest Life in Joy's eternal rest.

It will be real Life then, and worth the strife
We suffer now to fit our infant souls
To bear their part in that great world, which rolls
Always before us, great Eternity !
And all the labourers who have wrought with truth,
And those the sufferers who have bravely borne
Their share of earthly pain, will greet that morn
As toilers greet the night which brings them sleep,
And all the long-fought suffering, strong and deep,
Will find its purpose in that glorious Life.

The Supremacy of Man.

THE fairest flower that decks our mother earth
    Is but a flower, and thus it fades and dies;
Although the plant may bud and bloom again,
In quality it varies not, nor dwells
There in it any soul, nor higher life.
The lowest of created things that live,
The trees, the shrubs, the plants, wee flowerets, all
(Though of much value, and so beautiful)
Soon wither, and decay, and disappear;
And yet we would not underrate their charm,
Their sympathy, and more, their valued use.
Earth, with their many joys, is well-adorned;
Her soft green mantle, changing, ever fresh,
Starred with bright clusters of such varied hues,
The fairest, fragrant blossoms everywhere,
Is lovely in its beauty so superb;
And glorious are our noble, stately trees,
As, grandly waving in the rough, wild wind,
They bow their stalwart frames in honoured grace!
But noble, fair of aspect or of use,
As all this produce of dear Nature grows,
There still is lacking the great end of life,
The aspiring power, and this its brightest beam,
The hope of blessed immortality!

K

So with our beasts, though of a higher grade
Than simple plants, the brute creation still
Are but the second in development;
For Nature has three grades, apart from those
Which circle in the spirit world, and which
Are next to God, the Highest and Supreme,
Author of Nature, and the Lord of all;
And in these orders, those, the second, stand
Far in the ranks of lowly dignity;
High and yet low, because the space is vast
That marks the boundary 'twixt least and first.
Always supreme, king of the forest wilds,
The lion was, and is the monarch still;
But, noble Brute, with all thy sovereignty,
Thy stately mien, and strong majestic form,
Lion, thou king of beasts art but a brute,
And while our globe, our peopled sphere exists,
Thou canst not ever higher, nor wouldst thou, rise.

But *man*, ah, noble all-ambitious man,
Created in the like of God Himself,
Spiritual, blest with immortality,
What greater heights he can indeed attain!
His mighty deeds, so famous and so fair,
All those less famed, but not less beautiful;
The awful fires where martyrs for the Truth
In direst anguish slowly tasted death;
The noble sacrifice of all for Love,
And Faith, and Honour, and the lowly strain
Of self-denying lives for Duty spent;
The highest of the arts in deathless fame

Produced by mortal hearts, and heads, and hands
With patient labour ; and the grandest still,
The Incarnation of the Deity
Within the human clod of mortal frame,
These testify with uniform consent
To man's supremacy.   Within his breast
There dwells a soul, a strange mysterious soul,
A restless eager craving after life,
The highest, purest, noblest of existence ;
A wondrous yearning this, a beam Divine
That never shall be wholly quieted.
In some poor feeble frames, this takes the form
When left unsatisfied, of earthly lust,
In others 'tis a sordid mean ambition,
But never does the last spark flicker out
Of life's strange longing after fuller Life.
"Tis this which helps man onward in his race,
Sustaining him when other props give way ;
It is this great and glorious soul within
Which is the secret of his higher stand,
His sovereignty above the brutes and buds
Of God's creation.   Man is spiritual,
And he must rise beyond this dusky earth,
Even to Heaven itself ; for naught below
Should be the aim of his existence.   Nay,
Let nothing earthly e'er deter him, till
He gains the glorious goal he strives to win,
The measure of full life, the highest life,
Immortal, with a great Futurity !

Christmas Wishes.

WHAT message does Christmas-tide bring to you,
    O maid with the laughing eyes?
Does it whisper to you of a future fair,
Is it opening the way to the pleasures rare
Which you fancy are all awaiting you there
In the vista of coming years?
                And no fears
Enshadow the hue of the glorious view
The future presents, sweet maiden, to you;
But oh, my darling, take care, take care!
For the world holds many a hidden snare
Of which you know nothing, nor dream that sighs
And griefs will rob you of what you now prize,
Your beautiful youth; and in very truth
Your innocent sweetness is God's gift alone,
So cherish and keep it, a gem which to own
Many worldlings might vainly desire, in sooth.

And these are my wishes for you dear, to-day,
That all your fair life may be passed
If not in the sunshine, at least with content,
For in shadows the most peaceful years may be spent,
If over the darkness God's blessing is sent.
'Tis His Love that illumines our life,

And no strife
Can darken your way, if dear, as I pray
Your path has the joy I would wish you to-day.
Though sunshine and shadows may strangely be blent,
I trust that your path may be richly besprent
With the jewels of peace, and a calm that will last
No matter how rough or how wintry the blast.
Though your path may be long, may it never be wrong;
Let the trend of your life, dear, be always the right,
And there never shall fail you the clearest love-light
To enlighten the gloom in its hope full and strong.

And if with your dreams comes the sweet holy peace
Which Christmas joys often bring,
O spread, dear, around you this bright happy tide,
Those treasures with which you are richly supplied.
My darling, your sweetness and love do not hide,
But spread them the whole world around,
And abound
In love to increase, which never shall cease,
And scatter around us all goodwill and peace ;
And as love you may lavish on every side,
Sweet maiden, this love will still with you abide.
A paradox this, but a strange true thing,
That love nestles closely while yet on the wing,
And verily true.   Now darling, for you
I can wish nothing better this bright Christmas Day
Than that Love, Peace, and Gladness for ever will stay
To brighten your life, and bless all you may do.

The Evening Bell.

THE glorious sun is setting o'er the hill,
    The night keeps at a gracious distance still,
The air is full of calm and twilight peace,
All weary toilers now their tasks may cease,
For softly ringing through the meadowed dell
Is heard the music of the evening bell.

A noble ship is speeding o'er the main,
A sailor, wrapped in sleep, sees once again
The dear old homestead by the well-known wood,
He sees his mother where she last had stood
Whisp'ring goodbye; and 'mid the ocean's swell
He hears a sound as of the evening bell.

The city streets are thronged with motley crowd,
The strife is long, the tumult fierce and loud,
But soon there comes a hush amid the throng,
For is it not the hour for evensong?
And with the hush a sound comes like a spell,
The magic ringing of the evening bell.

That much-loved sound which in our dreams we hear,
Harmonious music ever sweet and clear
That in its ringing message carries rest,
Bringing a word of peace to souls distressed ;
What tales of joy and sorrow can it tell,
What stories long forgot, the evening bell !

Ring on then, tuneful bell, while earth shall last,
Bring peace to weary hearts till toil be past,
Ring on with joy throughout the summer's heat,
Ring gladly through the winter's snow and sleet ;
Ring on, fair chime, until the world's death knell
Shall take thy place, O blesséd evening bell.

Entered into Rest.

THE fainting breath is hushed at last,
   The weary form is sleeping,
Silently has the spirit passed
   Beyond our earthly keeping ;
      She has entered into rest !

Within the vail, her chastened soul
  Has gained the pastures vernal;
No more for her are tears and sighs,
Nothing but one sweet, long surprise,
  A joy supreme, eternal;
          She has entered into rest!

The parting smile of loving grace
  Is but a shadowy token
Of what her love can now embrace,
  Of what her heart has spoken;
          She has entered into rest!

The troubling cares which marked her path,
  The heavy clouds of sadness,
Are left below the dawning grey,
The night which yields to endless day,
  To everlasting gladness;
          She has entered into rest!

And seraphs chant their brightest songs,
  In joy at her returning
To meet the glad, beloved throngs,
  With eager rapture burning,
And all the earthly doubts and wrongs,
  The weary troubled yearning,
Have gently vanished from her breast,
Full joy is her's, redeemed and blest,
          She has entered into rest!

Christmas Melody.

HARK, 'tis the Christmas song !
   Now rising clear and strong,
And spreading holy peace the earth around ;
   The anthem of goodwill
   Echoes from hill to hill,
With earnest, joyously harmonious sound.

   This sweetest hymn of love,
   Trilled by the choirs above,
Soothes with its sweetness each poor troubled heart ;
   It thrills with lowly fear
   All who its music hear,
And lifts us grandly from the world apart.

   Hark, to the Christmas bells !
   The joyous music swells,
Gladly and gaily ring the cheerful peals ;
   Now softly sweet again,
   List to the peaceful strain
As calmly o'er our ears the chiming steals.

   The bells ring long and loud,
   Telling a world-worn crowd
That unto us a Saviour hath been born ;
   A glorious deed is done,
   God's Own Belovéd Son
Became Incarnate on this happy morn.

Sing on, ye voices sweet,
Ring on, O Bells, to greet
This festive Birthday of our gracious Lord,
And spread this Christmas tide
His tokens far and wide,
The "peace and goodwill" of His Holy Word.

A Farewell.

FAREWELL, the saddest word that may be spoken.
Farewell, whenever said, the tearful token
Of absence, short or long ; the saddest, yet
'Tis joined to deeper pain : Will they forget?

Forgotten ; ah, can Love e'er bear a sorrow
Worse than the pain our misery will borrow,
A fear of Memory once waxing cold,
A dread of newer ties o'ershadowing the old?

Farewell, so sad, and yet a word of blessing,
A God-speed, murmured by a voice caressing,
Which echoes grandly over land and sea,
That charms the heart with loving melody.

Farewell! Our Father lead you past all danger.
Farewell! His Love surround you, as, a stranger,
You launch in faith across a new life's way.
Farewell! May His grace guide and keep you every day!

The Story of the Christmas Rose.

THEY came, the Eastern Magi, to the humble
 stable door,
Which the Bethlehem Star illumined with its full and
 radiant store,
And beside the manger-cradle each in truest worship
 bowed,
As the royal Babe with costly gifts they willingly
 endowed.
The heavenly light shone o'er them, and revealed the
 happy grace
That spread in holy radiance across each dusky face,
And the silence of true worship marked their reverent
 attitude,
As they watched the noble Christ-child in the stable
 mean and rude.
Outside the lowly portal crouched a slight and girlish
 form,
Unmindful of the joy around, convulsed by inward
 storm,
And the grievous sobs which left her lips pierced
 through the deep blue skies,
As a torrent of long-gathered tears fell from her
 gleaming eyes.

The Baby-king of Heaven lay within that rough-built
    stall,
And the rich had gifts to offer in their love or great or
    small,
But she, in her deep reverence, the awe of earnest love,
Had not one gift to offer to the Child-king from above.
Hence then, her tears and sorrow, for her heart was
    torn with grief,
Till Heaven saw her trouble, and in mercy sent relief
Within the star's glad radiance an angel-form was seen,
So gentle its appearing, so comforting its mien,
No need to fear a visitant thus grandly bathed in light,
And the weeper's glistening tear-drops delayed their
    downward flight.
With a smile of sweet encouragement the Angel turned
    his head,
And bending o'er the wondering child he gently,
    softly said :
" My Daughter, why this sorrow? Do you fear the
    childlike King
" Doubts your love because you offer not the treasures
    others bring?
" If you welcome His glad coming, why deny it by
    your tears?
" Why clothe yourself in sorrow on the morn when
    He appears?
" Have a smile, child, for His welcome, show your
    heart's delight to Heaven,
" For your smile of treasured gladness is the greatest
    can be given.
" A lowly heart's devotion is a gift of wealth unknown

" Which our Father in His goodness loves to take and
    call His Own ;

" But He knows your heart craves something its sweet
    welcome to express,

" And reading your deep longing there, He willingly
    would bless

" And sanctify the sorrow which your love has caused
    to rise,

" In shewing forth His gracious power and tenderness
    of guise.

" In the pathway of this starlight blooms a fair and
    graceful flower,

" For its seed was cast from Heaven, and it grew amid
    the shower

" Of your own quick flowing tear-drops, those love-
    tokens of your heart

" As they fell beneath the star-beams of the traveller's
    brilliant chart.

" Like the Babe you hold in reverence, so this flower
    is pure and fair,

" Like the love your heart would offer, so the bloom
    is strangely rare,

" And the circling, golden stamens mark the wealth of
    love it brings

" To the treasury of its Master, earth's Emmanuel,
    King of kings,

" And its future shall betoken still the gradual growth
    of love,

" Till the highest Love shall conquer in its greater
    powers above."

So the childish heart found comfort in the Angel's
　　words of cheer,
As her wondering mind took in the thought of love
　　so full, so clear,
And the floweret in the pathway of the star-shine's
　　radiant light,
To her was still the lesson of the Christ-child's glad
　　Birth-night ;
And the lesson in its fulness, made her love *seem* poor
　　and cold,
But among the Master's treasures it shone brighter far
　　than gold.

A Beam of Light.

THE labour of the day was almost done,
　　The last few beams of the fair setting sun
Brightened my room, and one most glorious ray
Fell on the table where my Bible lay.
The Book, a birthday gift, was plainly bound
In dull, black leather, while the edges round
Were gilded, and reflected, strangely bright,
The sun-beams glittering in the ruby light.

A fitting circlet surely for God's word!
Thus musing, pure deep feelings in me stirred,
I uttered quietly the thought so sweet,
"Thy Word, Lord, is a lamp unto my feet."
And in my fancy, on that disc of gold
I saw the words in clear-writ letters bold,
And though they faded when the sun had set,
They linger with me in my memory yet.

They always bring me peace despite the care,
The sorrow that must come into my share,
And ever from that source so richly blest,
I take the joy that gives my spirit rest;
And when the Future sinks my heart with fear
I seek my God-lit lamp, whose love-beams clear
Reveal a blessing for the unknown path
That gives the promise for a glorious aftermath.

Winter Reveries.

I sit and I dream of the sunny skies
    And the orange groves of the Southern plain,
And the unbid tear dims my aching eyes,
    And there starts in my breast an unwonted pain.

I shiver beneath the chill winds of the North,
    Where the cold, grey clouds look cheerlessly down,
And the chary Sun peeps so rarely forth
    O'er the mighty city and murky town.

I watch the old Thames where the big ships glide,
    With its busy wharves and its countless piers,
And bitterly weep for the glowing tide
    Of the cherished sea of my youthful years.

By the shining strand I was wont to play
    With the eddies white from the curling blue ;
My home was the shore of that matchless Bay
    Where the sea meets sky in one blended hue.

The haunt above all where we loved to rove
    Was a winding path of exceeding grace,
Beneath the soft gloom of the deep cool grove
    Encircling the great Vesuvian base.

O ! The songs we trilled and the games we played,
   Outdoing the birds in our wild, young glee
As we danced and sang in the welcome shade,
   To the low sweet tones of the restless sea.

The world has evidenced many a change
   Since those happy hours of a day gone by,
And this life seems woefully hard and strange
   Through the worn-out disc of a feeble eye.

So I sit and think, and my only joy
   Is the favourite dream of the long ago,
Where the man is merged in the merry boy,
   And the city lost in the wavelet's flow ;

And an old man's faith in the dreams that bless
   Is helpful and sweet, for while Memory last
The grief of the Present grows faintly less
   In the radiance caught from the happy Past.

So I sit and dream, and I smile and weep ;
   I weep at the follies which seared my way,
But smile at the treasures these visions keep ;
   And weeping and smiling, I pass each day.

The Old Year and the New.

HOW strangely and softly the old year has sped
 Right away to the dim silent night,
The night of the Past to be never recalled
 With its burdens of wrong and of right ;
We search for it vainly, it cannot be found,
 Its redemption is out of our power ;
It silently passed, without even a sign,
 At the midnight's mysterious hour.

The old year is gone, its last moment is spent,
 The new year now greets us once more,
A year of fresh pathways for each, all untracked,
 And who knows what awaits him before ?
Ah, no one ! We welcome the opening year,
 But we know not what changes it holds,
Whether joys or deep sorrows are uppermost there,
 Whether life or still death it enfolds.

In ignorance, wondering, we meet it, in fear ;
 Maybe straining our dull bedimmed eyes
In vain hopes of catching some glimpse of our fate
 In the year that ahead of us lies.
We gaze, but we see not, the Future is blank,
 The near Present is only our own ;
The Past too is gone, and we only may use
 Just to-day's fleeting moments alone ;

Then oh, let us prize them, and use in good truth
　　Every moment we still may possess,
Remembering ever that Time must soon cease,
　　Each lost minute is making it less;
And all bravely girded to bear what of pain,
　　Or of pleasure the year has to give,
Prepared we shall be for whatever may come,
　　Be it death or a life yet to live.

Baby is in Heaven!

BABY is in Heaven! Weeping mother, dry your tears,
　　Your darling has a heritage for all the future
　　　years
Much brighter than the brightest which on earth he
　　might enjoy.
Weep not, mother; smile in faith o'er the gladness of
　　your boy.

Baby is in Heaven! He can see his Saviour's face,
His tiny form is beautified with such angelic grace,
His gentle heart is whiter than the purest snow-flake
　　known,
He sings among the angels standing round the Holy
　　Throne.

Baby is in Heaven ! He is waiting there for you,
Is resting near the golden gate, which you may soon
    pass through.
He opens wide his dear, sweet eyes, his lips curve
    with a smile ;
Is he thinking of his mother in th' little earthbound
    Isle ?

Baby is in Heaven ! You will join him by-and-bye,
Will meet him in the Kingdom spread so far beyond
    the sky,
And in the joy of meeting, you will soon forget all
    pain.
Weep not, mother ; trust in this : you will meet your
    boy again !

The Opium Slavery.

THE nineteenth century freedom,
    Is it altogether a dream ?
A beautiful myth of those idlers
    Who never will breast the stream ;
Who never will stem the current,
    'Gainst the flood of a drunken curse ;
Who would rather rest on the profits
    To be gained in the devil's purse ?

Why call yourselves free, my brothers,
  When our country's honour is seared
By as shameful a blot of slavery
  As ever on earth appeared?
Why pride yourselves on a nation
  Who will count in her treasure-hold
The millions won from a set of slaves,
  Whose enthraldom has made her gold?

Is ruin a work for Christians,
  A wreckage of body and soul?
Must we only stand idly waiting
  While sin gains the furthest goal?
While the dusky tribes of India,
  Our kin of the distant East,
Are slowly drawn into the vortex,
  The wallowing mire of the beast?

Will Englishmen yield their prestige
  For the sake of a paltry gain?
Shall their lust for the gold and silver
  Increase in its fearful bane?

*   *   *   *   *   *

Nay, surely our love for freedom
  Shall risk to condemn the deed
Which disgraces the prized escutcheon
  Of our land for a present greed;

And higher than all the honour
　We would bring to our country's name ;
Aye, and higher than all the motives
　For purging our land from shame,
Is the love of each earnest Christian
　Who would wave a fair, free sign
In the Name of the King of Nations
　O'er the light of an Eastern shrine !

The Shadow of the Cross.

UNDER the shadow of the Cross
　Where the pure sweet lilies grow,
Paled by the breath of woe
That darkly falls and coldly palls
Its anguished gloom on all below
In the shadow of the Cross.

Under the shadow of the Cross
Where Life strives long with death,
And Love with sin, in conflict stern and drear,
Where doubts creep in, yet vanquished, disappear
In the shadow of the Cross.

Under the shadow of the Cross
Where sorrow finds its depth,
Yet seeks its comfort there
Amid the clouds of care,
And seeking, finds the gain of loss
In the shadow of the Cross.

Under the shadow of the Cross
Where Love has conquered all,
Where death dethroned gives way to Life,
And Peace disperses fear and strife,
And Love alone is King of all
In the shadow of the Cross.

Over the shadow of the Cross
The beacon light of Love
Shines clearer for the deeper shade
That cowers below; and Love's pure glow
Beams out across a world of woe
In the shadow of the Cross.

The Flight of Time.

A moment lost!
Just one grain missed from Time's swift-dropping
    sands;
The shortest of all periods, but it stands
Before us now no longer.   It has passed,
    One moment lost.
Yet why regret the loss?   It is but slight,
A scarcely noticed token of Time's flight,
Only *one* moment passed into the night,
Only one moment passed into dull gloom,
Only a moment more to help our doom;
    One moment lost!

A minute lost!
An opportunity for lasting good
Missed in the leisure of weak hardihood,
Sent to the blameful records of the past,
    One minute lost.
But why disturb the present with regret?
The loss is trifling, we shall soon forget,
And charge our lapse of thought to Nature's debt;
Only one minute missing, let it rest;
It but awaits Eternity's behest,
    That minute lost.

An hour lost!
An hour passed in idle, fruitless play,
An hour wasted in our transient day,
Lost in the pursuit of a worthless scheme,

One hour lost ;
Gone to increase the swelling, mighty store
Of moments lying on th' Eternal Shore,
The wasted minutes of the days of yore ;
But why this trouble?   Only one short hour
Taken for ever from our service power ;
One hour lost !

A work-day lost !
Missed from the gathering echoes of the year,
Missed—how or when may not at once appear,
But missing still it lies amid our past,
A work-day lost.
Missed, maybe, in that hour we fraught with schemes,
Missed in that moment spent in idle dreams,
Lost through a minute ; ah, how strange it seems !
But only *one* day spent, and life is long ;
We still have years before us, we are strong ;
Just one day lost.

A life-time lost !
The breath is feeble, and the frame is worn,
The soul may never know the years unborn,
Even the present holds but useless hours ;
A life-time lost ;
Lost in the moments of a careless ease,
Spent in an hour's vain toils ourselves to please ;
Stranded for ever from our life's high seas
The wasted moments of the days now past
Rise to condemn us with their shame at last ;
A life-time lost !

M

And there was no more Sea.

(REV. XXI, 1).

THE splash of the musical waters falling sweetly on
    the ear,
And the scent of the ocean breezes with their gentle
    rustlings near;
Above, the cloud-hung sky-roof in its drapings of
    silver grey
Broken, here and there, for the azure to brighten the
    summer day;

It is here that the Soul's great yearning springs on to
    the end of life,
The temporal life of the earth child, with its tumult of
    wearying strife,
Springs up to the great Forever when all these shall
    cease to be,
When the vision shall be completed: "And there
    was no more sea."

No heaping of troubled billows to buffet the fainting
    soul,
No snares to wreck the unwary where the great waves
    break and roll,
No darkly hidden caverns where misery dwells alone,
Where the depths may never be sounded of the woe
    its sorrows own.

Here the splash of the musical waters may rise to an
    angry roar,
With the strife of the wind in its fury to lash it along
    the shore,
And the silvery blue of the heav'ns may be darkened
    with sudden gloom,
The portent of darker shadows in many a sea-laid
    tomb.

But there in the long Hereafter, where the song of the
    waves must cease,
The roar and the thunderous breaking must also give
    way to peace,
A calm of the fairest summer, the repose of the only
    rest,
The end of Life's Sea with the tumults it carries across
    its breast.

So we may not waste our sighing for the sea we have
    learnt to love,
Because we can never meet it in our truest Life Above
Where the restless, troubled ocean must ever cease
    to be,
For within the Peace of the perfect Life there shall
    be " no more Sea."

www.ingramcontent.com/pod-product-compliance
Lightning Source LLC
Chambersburg PA
CBHW021113020726
47500CB00003B/736